FIRE OVER ATLANTA

Bonnets and Bugles Series · 9

FIRE OVER ATLANTA

GILBERT MORRIS

MOODY PRESS

CHICAGO

YA
MOR

ISBN: 0-8024-0919-9

1 3 5 7 9 10 8 6 4 2

Printed in the United States of America

*To Sue Branstetter—the best typist
and researcher on the planet!!!*

Contents

1
Leah Makes a Decision

With a grunt, Leah Carter tugged at the buttons on the back of her dress. She struggled so violently that her face turned red, but no matter how hard she tried she simply could not fasten the garment.

"I'm getting to be nothing but a great big cow!" In a gesture of despair, Leah ran her hands through her blonde hair and stared at her image in the mirror. "Nothing but a big cow!"

Her full lower lip extended in a pout. Impatiently she pulled the dress over her head, held it up, stared at it angrily. She knew that it was foolish to be angry at the dress.

She glanced then at the homemade calendar on the wall and noted the date. June 20, 1864. The memory of that day a year ago came to her, and she lowered the dress slowly and sat down on the edge of the bed. The cornshuck mattress whispered and rustled.

"It was just a year ago today that I got this dress," she whispered. "I was so proud of it—and Jeff was too." She held up the garment. It was royal blue with beautifully executed bone buttons at the back, white cuffs, and a white collar to match. She remembered how Jeff had taken her for a walk down the streets of Richmond and how he had whispered, "You're the prettiest girl in Richmond, Leah Carter!"

As Leah remembered, a dreamy look came into her blue-green eyes. She thought of Jeff Majors and wished that the dress still fit.

Then she thought of the party she was invited to at Lucy Driscoll's house tonight, and she threw the dress across the room. It sailed through the air, hit the wall, and dropped in a crumpled heap on the worn, blue-figured carpet.

Leah walked around the confines of her small bedroom, coming finally to stand at the window. She stared at the tall oaks lining the dusty road that led to Richmond in one direction and to the Driscoll house in the other. It was a fine day, and soon Jeff would be coming down that road to take her to Lucy's party. She felt a sudden twinge of jealousy.

"I bet Lucy will have a dress sent all the way from France on one of the blockade runners," she muttered. She turned from the window, walked over to the large, polished, walnut wardrobe, and stared inside again, although she knew it was hopeless. She pawed through her few dresses and wished that she had the green dress that she had left at her home back in Kentucky. And then she shook her head. *That one would be too small too!*

The big black-and-white cat lying in the center of her bed lifted his massive head and looked at her with golden eyes. He said, "Wow?" which always made Leah laugh.

She laughed now. Then she fell across the bed and ran her hand over the cat's smooth, glossy fur. "You're all right, Cap'n Brown!" she said. He seemed to be wearing a black-and-white suit with the white of his neck forming a white cravat. He had been

10

placed in the barn to catch rats and mice, but Leah had taken him into the house and for some reason had decided to call him Cap'n Brown. She picked up the cat, and he purred as she stroked his ebony fur, lifting his head to be tickled under his chin. "I know what you want," she said. "You want to be brushed."

"Wow," Cap'n Brown said, and Leah again laughed. She found his brush and began giving him long, easy strokes. Cap'n Brown arched his back with pleasure as the brush traveled down his lanky body.

"I wish my hair were as easy to fix as yours," she said, reaching up to touch her blonde locks. She had washed her hair with rainwater just that morning, and it was still slightly damp, the ends of it curling. She realized that she had to do something with it.

"I can't be brushing you all the time, Cap'n Brown." She tossed him off her lap.

He landed lightly on the bed, stared at her, then yawned and curled up and immediately went to sleep.

With a sigh, Leah went back to the wardrobe and chose the only dress that would do at all for the party. It was one she had made only four weeks earlier, so she knew the fit was right. The trouble was that it was not intended to be a party dress.

She held it up to the light. "It's just a plain, old brown dress," she said, "but it's either that or wear overalls." Quickly she slipped it on, looking longingly again at the royal blue dress that was so pretty.

She sat down then at the little desk beside her spool bed and pulled a small book toward her. This was the journal for which she had spent twenty-five Confederate dollars earlier in the year. If I were

11

buying it now, she thought, it would cost fifty dollars or seventy-five or perhaps even a hundred. Confederate money was practically worthless.

"I'm glad I bought it when I did," she murmured, then dipped a quill into the glass inkwell and began to write. It was a pleasure to write in her journal, and she loved looking back and seeing what she had been thinking six months ago. Some of it made her laugh, and other writing embarrassed her for she was able to see her own foolishness.

The turkey quill scratched across the page as Leah wrote in tiny, ornate script, dipping the pen from time to time into the ink, which also was growing scarce. She stopped after a time and reread what she had written:

> Am I a girl—or am I a woman? Just now I tried on the blue dress that fit me perfectly a year ago, but now I can't even squeeze into it. I'm no taller than I was then, and I thank the Lord for that! I'm tall enough already at five feet seven, which is plenty. But I've filled out so that I've got to wear my brown dress, and it was never meant for a party. But I'm going to Lucy's party, no matter what!

She sat at the desk, dreamily thinking of what her life had been like. Looking back through the journal, she saw entries about things that had taken place when she was at home with her family in Pineville. She read again, with pleasure, about bringing Jeff's baby sister, Esther, to be with his family here in Richmond.

She read references to the Majors family and to Jeff himself, who had been her best friend all her life.

12

They had the same birthday, and now Leah thought of how Jeff, at eighteen, had changed from a lanky, wild-haired boy to a fine-looking man like his father, Col. Nelson Majors, and like his older brother, Tom.

The Majors family had moved South at the beginning of the Civil War. Then Colonel Majors's wife died, leaving the small child that she named Esther. And now the three Majors men were all in Richmond with the Confederate army.

Leah's lips curled upward as she thought of baby Esther, whom she had cared for and who had taken up so much of her life. Not a baby now, for she was three years old and talking more every day.

She thought also of the future. Colonel Majors and Eileen Fremont planned to be married soon, and Esther would have a new mother. Jeff, at first, had been opposed to his father's taking another wife. But he had come around and now seemed to love Eileen Fremont as much as he had disliked her before.

Leah began to write again:

I know that Lucy will have a beautiful dress, and she's so little and pretty that she makes me look even more gawky and bigger than I am. And Jeff, he's just like all the rest of the boys. Just dazzled by Lucy. What chance do I have? I'll have to wear a dress that isn't pretty, and I won't get to dance a single time with Jeff, and I'll just sit in a corner, and nobody will even notice me!

Slowly Leah leaned back, wiped the quill on a piece of cloth kept for that purpose, and put the brass cap on the ink bottle. She sprinkled a little fine, white sand over the writing to dry it, blew it off, and then read what she had written. Something about it, she knew, was wrong, but she could not understand what. What she thought was, *I'm seventeen years old, and that's a woman—but sometimes I don't feel grown up. So what am I? A little girl or a woman?*

The Driscoll home was ornate, large, beautiful, and, Leah knew, filled with expensive paintings and decorations. As Jeff stopped the team in front of the big portico with its eight white columns, again she felt intimidated by it all. She watched as a tall slave came out and took the lines from Jeff.

The man flashed his white teeth. "Yes, suh, I will take care of this team. The party's startin'. You better get on in!"

"Thanks." Jeff got down and went around to Leah's side and put up a hand.

She took it, noting that he looked very handsome indeed in his ash-gray Confederate uniform. He had begun the war as a drummer boy at Bull Run but now was a full-fledged private in the Stonewall Brigade. His black belt and boots and the red sash around his trim middle made him look very athletic. She glanced at his hair, the blackest she had ever seen, and thought again, *He's the best-looking boy I've ever known.*

All the way to the Driscoll house, Jeff had talked about going back to duty. He still moved his left arm rather awkwardly, for he had been slightly wounded at the siege of Petersburg. General Grant, with thousands of Federal soldiers, was still drawn up in front of that city, and the Confederates were fighting in a desperate attempt to keep them from coming through and taking Richmond.

14

However, Jeff now seemed able to put this from his mind. His grin flashed, and he held Leah's hand for just a moment longer than necessary, leaning over to wink at her. "You're going to have a good time at this party," he promised. "Everybody will be here."

Leah smiled quickly. "I hope so, Jeff. Don't leave me all alone, now."

"Oh, you won't need me. There'll be plenty of fellas coming to ask you to dance. Let's go in."

Leah and Jeff entered the palatial mansion and moved down the hall toward the sound of music. When they stepped into the ballroom, she saw that the large room was filled with young people and decorations hung from the chandeliers and on the walls. Across one end stood a long table, draped with a white cloth and topped with gleaming china. Cut crystal glasses caught and reflected the light from the chandeliers.

The dancing had already started, for Lucy Driscoll would have nothing less for her birthday than a dance. The music was provided by a five-piece band, and the dresses of the young women looked like green, red, blue, and yellow lights as they moved about the room.

"This beats starving in the trenches at Petersburg," Jeff said. Then his eyes narrowed. "There's Lucy."

As Leah had guessed, the girl was wearing the most beautiful gown that money could buy. Lucy's dress was baby blue silk with a small, woven floral design. It had a square neckline, edged with a white lace frill. The lace-frilled sleeves were very short and puffed. The overskirt touched the floor and was looped up at the sides and held in place by large

15

white silk bows. It was worn over a large hoop. Her fair hair was coiled high on her head with long ringlets hanging down the back. She had on short, white silk gloves and a pearl choker.

"Let's go wish her a happy birthday," Jeff said.

Leah seized Jeff's arm and clung to him. She had the impulse to turn and run, for she felt like a crow at a meeting of brilliantly colored bluejays and cardinals and canaries. Her brown dress, though serviceable enough for church, was totally out of place here. She wanted to cry.

I wish I'd never come, she thought and gritted her teeth. *As soon as I can, I'll get away where nobody can see me.*

"Why, Jeff, how nice to see you—and you too, Leah."

Lucy Driscoll was small and shapely and charming. Her hair was as blonde as Leah's, but whereas Leah was tall and strong-looking, Lucy was diminutive and made the most of it.

"You look great, Lucy." Jeff smiled, taking her hand. He bent over and kissed it, then laughed. "I been practicing up on that."

"I bet it was with Leah here," Lucy said archly. "Has he been practicing his charms on you, Leah?"

"No," Leah said shortly, "he hasn't!"

Jeff shifted uncomfortably. "To tell the truth, that was my first attempt. Anyway, I been practicing up on my dancin', even though it was all by myself." The music started up again just then, and he said, "Could I have this dance, Lucy?"

"Oh, I'm sorry. I already promised it to Cecil."

A thin young man about Jeff's age, who had been standing off to one side listening, stepped forward. He had chestnut hair and bright eyes and wore the uniform of a first lieutenant. "Go ahead. I'll make the sacrifice for you, Jeff."

"Well, that's nice of you, Cecil—I mean, lieutenant. I keep forgetting you've been commissioned, sir."

"Oh, let's forget that," Cecil said, "at least while we're here." He seemed to be the only officer present among several young soldiers and many civilian boys not yet old enough to enlist. He turned to Leah. "May I have this dance, Leah?"

Glad to get away and feeling very warm toward the young man, Leah said, "Of course." She soon was sweeping around in a waltz with Cecil Taylor. He was not the best of dancers, but she liked him.

"Sorry about that," he said after a misstep. "I'm just never going to learn to be good at this."

Leah smiled at him. "You're doing fine."

Cecil was only an inch or two taller than Leah herself. She had grown fond of him on her first trip to Richmond. At that time he had proved to be a friend when Lucy had been somewhat less than friendly. His father was a wealthy planter. His mother was from one of the finest—that is to say, wealthiest—families of Virginia.

Leah glanced around the ballroom. "There aren't as many here as I thought there would be," she remarked.

"No, it's not like it used to be. I remember when fellows would come from all over the county for a party like this. But I guess a lot of 'em are in the army now. And besides, there just aren't enough horses to get us where we want to go." He looked down at her, interest in his friendly blue eyes. "I'm so glad you could come," he said. "I was afraid you might have gone back to Kentucky."

17

"I suppose I'll have to pretty soon. I came to bring Jeff's little sister here, but now that it looks like his father's going to remarry, they won't need me anymore as a nurse for her."

"That'll be a sorry day for me when you go back. As a matter of fact, I've missed you a lot."

"Will you be in the fighting soon?"

"I don't know. I've put in for it, but they keep me here as an aide in the War Department." Cecil sounded disgusted, and he missed another step, almost stumbling. "Sorry about that."

"What do you hear from your brother, Royal?" he asked after the music stopped and they were at the refreshment table. He was pouring her some lemonade from a tall pitcher.

Leah said, "He's in Chattanooga, but I don't think you'd want to hear about the doings of a Yankee soldier."

"If he's your brother, I would!" Cecil sipped his lemonade and made a face. "This doesn't have enough sugar in it. Here, let's sweeten it up with some of these cakes." He picked up some small white cakes coated with sugar and bit into one. "The Yankees whipped us pretty bad at Chattanooga, but I don't think they'll ever take Atlanta."

"I just wish it was over," Leah said, "and that we didn't have to hear about war all the time."

Across the ballroom, Jeff stood talking to Lucy. He was enjoying himself tremendously. He was also looking forward to having some of the refreshments, for food had gotten scarce in the Confederacy. Looking down at Lucy, he said, "That's the prettiest dress I've ever seen, I think. You sure look nice."

"Why, thank you, Jeff."

"I haven't seen you wear that one before."

"No, it came in on a privateer last month. Daddy bought it for me. Had to pay too much for it, I think."

"It was worth it." He led her toward the refreshment table. "Sure wish there wasn't anything to do but go to parties, and drink lemonade, and eat cake. Sure beats soldiering."

"Leah looks nice," Lucy said idly.

"What? Oh, yes, she does."

"She's so tall, though. I hope she doesn't grow any taller."

"I don't know. She looks pretty healthy."

"Oh, yes, she's healthy all right. Look, she and Cecil are trying to dance again. Cecil isn't much on a dance floor, I'm afraid."

Jeff glanced over as Cecil almost tripped over Leah's long skirt.

Lucy said, "Well, I hope he doesn't fall down and drag Leah with him. That would humiliate her, wouldn't it . . ."

"This is too much to ask a lady to put up with," Cecil said.

Leah was somewhat embarrassed, but she said, "No, you're not going to get any better if you don't practice."

The evening went on and on, and Lucy and Jeff —it seemed to Leah—danced almost every dance together. She herself kept going back to Cecil, who stood much of the time against the wall. "Come along, Cecil," she would say, taking his hand.

The more she saw Jeff laughing down at Lucy Driscoll, the more unhappy she became. *If I can't have the prettiest dress, I'll have to do something else to get Jeff's attention,* she thought.

Leah was not a scheming girl. But having come to the party in such poor style, and then seeing Jeff so taken with Lucy Driscoll, she decided that she had to do something. She toyed with an idea. *If he's going to pay all that much attention to Lucy, then I'm going to make him jealous. I'll make him jealous of Cecil.*

The thought pleased her, and she moved closer to Cecil, saying, "You do look nice in your uniform, Cecil. I think officers of the Confederacy are so dashing, and I'm sure you're going to be a perfect hero when you get your chance."

Leah had never paid such attention to Cecil before, and he seemed dazzled by her compliments. "Why, Leah, I didn't know you felt like that!"

"Oh, I do! Now, let's try again. One, two, three. One, two, three. That's it! You're going to be the best dancer when I get through with you, Cecil Taylor."

Leah hardly saw the pleased look that came into Cecil's eyes. She looked across the room at Jeff and Lucy, thinking, *I'll make him so jealous, he won't even see Lucy Driscoll.*

2
Friends Fall Out

Sgt. Royal Carter entered the tent and found Pvt. A. B. Rose lying limply on his cot.

"What's the matter with you, Rosie?" Royal said. "You're not ready for breakfast?"

For a moment the gangling soldier stretched out on the cot said nothing. Then he looked past his big feet to reveal a pair of light blue eyes. His tow-colored hair was badly awry. He managed to say mournfully, "Well, sergeant, I reckon my time has come."

"The time's come for breakfast!"

Rosie shook his head. "Nope, it's all up with me this time, Royal. I don't hold out much hope that I can make it anymore."

"What's wrong with you?" Royal stood over him. "You look all right to me."

"Well, looks are plumb deceivin'. You ought to know that. I might look good, but I ain't good inside. No, sir, not a bit of it!"

A slight smile curled the corners of Royal Carter's lips. He mused over the limp figure of the tall private a moment more. "Well," he said, "if you feel so bad, I guess I'd better go and eat those pancakes and ham that the cooks made for us this morning."

As Royal had anticipated, the mention of pancakes seemed to bring fresh strength into Rosie. He sat up at once, cleared his throat, and ran his hands through his hair. "Well, now, Professor—maybe if you'll help me, I can make it to the mess hall. Then

21

if I get one of those pancakes down me, I might feel better."

"Just lean on me, Rosie," Royal said soothingly. Hiding a grin, he pretended to sag as the huge private put an arm over his shoulder and the two started for the eating area.

Royal, at twenty-two, was not more than five feet nine but was sturdy and strong. He had light hair and blue eyes and was known as Professor by his fellow soldiers primarily because he had some college education. He also was rarely seen without a book.

The mess hall was a large frame building that had once been a factory but had been seized by the Federal army when it took Chattanooga. It had been turned into a fine kitchen and mess hall combined.

"Come on, now! You're going to make it! Just up these steps."

Hanging on loosely and shuffling his feet, Rosie said, "I made my will out last night."

"Again? That's the tenth will you've made that I know of! I wish I was as sure of living as you are, Rosie. You're healthy as a horse."

Rosie's craggy features looked pained. "Nobody understands me," he said. "I'm a sick man."

Actually there was no healthier soldier in the Union army than Pvt. A. B. Rose. He was indeed healthy as a horse and as strong as one as well. But he fancied himself sick and repeatedly went to the surgeon of the regiment, trying to explain his ailments. He had an enormous collection of patent medicines, including pills, syrups, and concoctions of all sorts, to which he added some that he himself had invented. His friends warned him that he was going to kill himself with some of these medicines, but Rosie gloomily persisted.

The two soldiers went into the mess hall, and Royal called out, "Make room, men! Let's help poor old Rosie try to hold something down."

A yell went up from the soldiers, who were putting away pancakes at a prodigious rate.

Walter Beddows, a short, stocky boy with brown hair and brown eyes, laughed aloud. "Sit down here by me, Rosie. I'll hold you up while Sergeant Pickens stuffs a few pancakes down your throat."

Another private said, "Here, I'll even pour the syrup on 'em. We got fresh-made sorghum."

Rosie sat and looked across the table at Walter and Ira Pickens, a tall, lean sergeant with brown eyes and bushy black hair, who grinned at him.

"I think he's gonna die this time, Ira," Walter said.

"No, just get some of these pancakes down him. They'd make a corpse come to life."

A great deal of wry humor passed back and forth as Rosie slowly forked a pancake onto his plate. He drowned it in syrup, cut it in two, and stuffed half of it into his mouth. Then he annihilated the second half. His eyes brightened. "That's better, fellas. Let me have a few more of those."

Royal watched and winked at his fellow sergeant, Ira Pickens, as Rosie helped himself to a half dozen large pancakes and attacked them.

"I suppose you're going to live, aren't you, Rosie?" Ira asked finally.

"I reckon I will. If I just had some coffee and a piece of that ham to come out even."

Rosie looked up as another private entered. The newcomer was tall, strong-looking, athletic. He had crisp brown hair, gray eyes, and his uniform was spotless. "Well, Drake, I think I'm going to make it. These pancakes, I believe, have got some kind of therapeutic value."

Drake Bedford took a seat and lifted his eyebrows at Rosie. They had joined up together and were the best of friends. "You didn't leave any pancakes for me?" he exclaimed. "What a pig!"

"Here," Royal said, "I saved three of them back for you."

"Hey, thanks a lot, sergeant." Drake grinned. "I'll do the same for you sometime."

As Drake began eating his pancakes, talk went around the table about the battle that they had just been through.

"We sure whipped them Rebs this time!" somebody said. "I reckon the Army of Tennessee is running yet after we charged 'em up Missionary Ridge."

Loud cries of agreement sounded, and Walter Beddows said, "You're right about that. Furthermore, I think we're gonna run 'em all the way back to Atlanta."

"It's about time we won a battle," Sergeant Pickens put in. He was a homely young man, a good friend of Leah Carter, and somewhat struck with her. He winked at Royal. "I got me a letter from your sister Leah."

Royal grinned. "Are you still tryin' to court her? I told you—she's dotty about Jeff Majors."

"He's just an old Confederate," Ira drawled. "Just let me get close to her again, and I'll show you what courtin' really is."

Some catcalls went up at this.

And then Walter Beddows winked at Rosie and said, "Hey, Drake, how you doin' with *your* courtin'?"

Drake had been eating steadily, but at Walter's remark his face assumed a frown. "I'm doin' all right," he said.

"Is that right?" Walter continued. He loved to tease. "Why, I heard our sergeant has the inside track on that little ol' Lori Jenkins."

"Cut it out, will you, Walter!" Royal said. He and Drake were competing for Lori Jenkins's hand, and he knew that Drake hated to be teased.

But Walter never knew when to stop, and he kept up his teasing until finally Drake said, "Beddows, shut up, or I'll clean your plow!"

"Oh, he didn't mean anything," Royal said quickly. He hated to see dissension among his squad and shot a warning frown at Walter.

Drake, however, was extrasensitive. He got up and walked stiffly out of the mess hall.

"Hey, you left your pancakes!" Rosie called after him. "Do you mind if I have 'em?"

Drake went out, slamming the door.

"Whooie, he sure is powerful touchy, isn't he, Professor?" Walter said.

"Too touchy—and you fellows lay off of him! You hear me? Especially you, Walter. You never know when to quit."

Rosie commandeered the remains of Drake's breakfast and consumed them with relish. "You're right about that, Professor. I've known Drake a long time. If he didn't have such a hot temper, he'd live longer. I been tellin' him he ought to take some of my liver pills." He swallowed the last bite and sighed with satisfaction. "Come to think of it, I better take some myself." He reached into his pocket and pulled out a huge bottle. He removed the top and shook out a handful of pills. "You fellows want some?" he asked. Getting no takers, he took two and swallowed them easily without water. "Now," he said, "that ought to calm my innards down a little bit."

"They better be calm because we're gonna be headin' out of here any time," Royal said.

"General Sherman tell you that?" Pickens asked with a grin.

"Everybody knows about it. We'll be headin' for Atlanta, and there'll be plenty of fightin' along the way."

After the Confederates retreated from Chattanooga, General Sherman at once gave orders to follow them. He had three armies, 110,000 men strong; Gen. Joe E. Johnston's Army of Tennessee had fewer than 65,000. The Union troops packed up and started out toward Atlanta.

During the march, Rosie asked, "What do you think about our strategy, Royal? How are we goin' to whip them Rebs?"

The others listened avidly, for Royal was the only man in the squad who paid much attention to strategy.

"Well," he said, "we've got to do two things. First, we've got to whip Johnston's army. And the second thing is, we've got to capture Atlanta."

"Why do we need Atlanta?" Drake muttered sourly.

Royal pretended not to notice Drake's sullen looks. He knew Drake did not like soldiering. "Next to Richmond," he said, "Atlanta is the most important manufacturing city in the South. If we can capture that, that'll reduce their ability to wage war. They won't have anything left to fight with."

"What do you think the Confederates are going to do?" Walter Beddows asked.

"First they're going to try and whip us. But being so outnumbered, I don't think they can handle that," Royal said. "I think they'll retreat and try to trick us into some ground where they'll have more of a chance. And, of course, secondly, they'll hole up and defend Atlanta. But you know what they're really tryin' to do is stall for time."

"Why they doin' that?" Rosie inquired.

"Because, if the war keeps on going on, some of our folks back home might decide it costs too much. And if President Lincoln gets defeated next November, the war might just be stopped. So if they can just hold out, they've got a good chance of winning that way."

The others listened, but Royal knew they actually paid little attention to theories.

However, they soon paid attention to the action. When the Federals arrived at a place called Resaca, they made an attack, and there was intense fighting. After this, they pursued the Rebels until they fought again. Johnston and his Confederate forces were waiting for them at Newhope Church, and hard battles were fought there.

Royal and his squad were sent on a wide, ranging sweep and, after a series of operations, found themselves in front of Kennesaw Mountain. The Northern army had come three-fourths of the way to Atlanta, and so far there had been only isolated pitched battles. But this time Sherman loosed the entire Federal force on Confederate positions.

Sherman's troops took considerable mauling, and the general, fighter that he was, decided that Atlanta could not be taken by a frontal assault. The Union forces then moved along the Chattahoochee River, and the Confederates eventually retired across the river to a strong position just north of Atlanta.

During all of the battles, Drake had fought with courage. He was a man who could endure almost anything except inactivity. He was a social being, loved parties, played the fiddle well, had a good singing voice, and had been very popular in civilian life. Now, once the armies were not fighting but simply waiting it out, he became restless.

Royal was careful how he spoke to Drake. He considered the man a friend even though the two of them were in fierce competition for Lori Jenkins. But being a responsible sergeant, finally he could overlook Drake's malingering and laziness no longer. Approaching him one morning as Drake lay outside his tent while the other men were working, he said, "Drake, up and at it! Help the other fellas!"

Drake, unfortunately, had found some liquor the night before and had gotten drunk. He probably had a terrible headache, for he flinched at the impact of Royal's voice. Without opening his eyes he said, "You don't need me, Royal!"

Even as he spoke, an officer walked by, Lt. Harvey Logan, a hard man on any private who spoke back to his officer or noncom.

Alarmed, Royal said, "Come on, Drake, get with it!"

Drake, again without opening his eyes, cursed Royal and told him, "Get away and leave me alone!"

"On your feet, private!"

At the rough voice of the lieutenant, Drake did open his eyes, and when he saw the anger on Logan's face, he scrambled to his feet.

"If you don't like to work, I'll give you something better to do."

"I think I can discipline him, lieutenant," Royal said hastily. "If you don't mind, sir."

"I do mind!" the lieutenant said. "He's been getting away with murder! Let him ride the horse. See if he likes that. After a few hours, he'll be glad to go to work."

The rest of the squad stood listening to all this, and some of them looked pleased. Royal knew they resented having to do Drake's work.

"Get him on that horse!"

Royal had no choice. "Come on, Private Bedford."

Drake had gone too far, but he was a proud young man and would never beg. When he got to the wooden "horse," which was a rough pole six inches across and suspended six feet in the air by crossed legs, he turned a little pale. Men had been kept straddled on this apparatus until they cried for mercy.

"On that pole, Bedford," Lieutenant Logan ordered.

Drake leaped up and straddled the pole. He held on with his hands in front of him and waited.

"Tie his feet under there!" Lieutenant Logan said, and with regret Royal obeyed the order.

"How long do I have to stay up here, sir?"

"I'll tell you when you can get down! You can think about what a sorry soldier you are while you're up there!" Lieutenant Logan gave Royal a hard glance. "You leave him there, sergeant, until I tell you to take him down."

"Yes, sir!"

For the next six hours, Drake sat on the horse.

What was at first uncomfortable became literal torture after a while. He tried to shift his position, raising himself off the pole from time to time. But that was impossible for long.

Even worse than the torture were the snickers and laughter of the men of A Company who came by. "Ride 'em, cowboy!" they would yell. "You got him, Drake! Just ride him all the way back to Washington!" Such gibes infuriated him, but he could not do anything about it.

The lieutenant came by at dusk. "All right, sergeant, cut him loose."

Royal slit the thongs binding Drake's feet and said, "Let me help you down, Drake."

"Get away from me!" Drake slipped off the pole, clinging to it to keep from falling until the circulation came back to his legs. Then he staggered off, his face set in an air of resentment.

"He sure doesn't learn very good, does he, Professor?" Jay Walters remarked.

"He sure don't!" Rosie put in. "He's always shootin' himself in the foot. Sure wish he would learn to be nice and easygoing. Maybe some of this new syrup I made out of hemlock will help him."

Jay shook his head. "I don't think any medicine is gonna help him. Just a change of heart."

"He needs that all right. He's a right good feller. He's just got too much temper for one man."

3

Drake Sees a Miracle

The road to Atlanta wore the Union army threadbare. Day by day the troops slogged forward, fighting battle after battle. The Confederates, led by the wily General Johnston, fought a masterful withdrawal. It was said of Johnston that on retreat he was like a savage wolf, the best general in either army at such tactics.

After many nasty little battles, Royal Carter sat in front of a sputtering campfire, studying the squad that he was charged with leading. A cold rain was falling, and the fire over which Royal and Walter Beddows were trying to cook bacon and make johnnycakes was a miserable failure.

"I'm tired of all this!" Walter complained. He suddenly sat back, and the muddy ground squished beneath him. "We fight, and fight, and fight—and those blasted Rebels just back up and hit us again from the sides!"

Walter had a tin plate in his hand and was hungrily awaiting breakfast. Now he pulled his poncho around his shoulders and tilted his forage cap forward so that the water ran down on his shirtfront. "I'd just as soon bore through to China as get to Atlanta."

"It's not so bad," Royal said quickly, trying to keep up the spirits of his men. "We'll make it, fellas. We just have to keep plugging."

Drake and Rosie were staring morosely at the sorry attempts to put breakfast together. Rosie said, "If I don't get some more of my liver medicine pretty soon, I'm going to die before I can get shot."

"Well, if you die of liver trouble, you won't have to worry about gettin' shot!" Drake said irritably. He looked up at the sullen, gray sky where dark clouds rolled in huge thunderheads, some scattering as a wild wind drove them apart. "I wish this blamed *rain* would clear up!"

"It'll probably clear off soon," Royal said. "Let's get some dry firewood under here and see if we can get this breakfast going."

The squad struggled for some time to get their breakfast cooked but finally succeeded. They sat around eating hotcakes and bacon, and the rain did turn into a fine mist that soaked into their already sodden clothing. They were almost finished with the meal when Major Bates strolled past with several of his officers.

He looked purposeful, and Royal perked up at once. "It looks like there's going to be some action," he said.

"I hope not," Rosie groaned. "My rheumatism's acting up."

Despite Rosie's professed rheumatism, Royal saw the officers go off to Sherman's headquarters.

That afternoon, Royal looked up to see Lieutenant Logan walking toward them. "He looks like he means business, doesn't he, Walter?"

"Sure does," Beddows said, "and I don't like it when officers look like that. It means trouble for us."

"Sergeant," Lieutenant Logan said, stopping before Royal and Beddows. "We're going to be attacking in the morning. I want every man in your squad to carry a full pack, three days' rations, and keep your powder dry."

"What are we going to do, lieutenant?" Royal asked.

"I expect we're going to hit the Rebels hard and wade right into Atlanta. Be sure the men are ready at dawn."

Royal thought Lieutenant Logan looked half angry. He must have disagreed with his superior officers about the manner of attack and had been overruled, being merely a lowly lieutenant.

"I guess we'd better tell the rest of the fellas," Royal said. He and Beddows gathered the squad together, and Royal said as cheerfully as possible, "We'll be attacking in the morning. Going to take Atlanta this time."

"Take Atlanta!" Drake stared at him. "Whose bright idea was that?"

"General Sherman's, I suppose, Drake."

"Well, it doesn't make no sense." Drake shook his head. "We've been nibblin' away at the Rebels every day, and the harder we fight, the more they fight back. And now we're going to try a head-on attack? It's stupid!"

"It's orders!" Royal said sharply. "Everybody get your equipment together. Be sure you've got plenty of ammunition. We'll be leaving at daylight."

"I got half a mind to turn myself in sick," Drake muttered.

"I feel the same way," Rosie said, "but I been on sick call so much they wouldn't believe me. You can do it though, Drake. You ain't never reported in sick."

"Nope! If we're gonna be fools, I'll be a fool with the rest of you!" He suddenly grinned, reached over, and slapped his tall, towheaded friend on the back. "I got to look out for you, don't I? I declare, you wouldn't last a day without me!"

Dawn came, and it was a beautiful morning. The squad ate together as the yellow light in the east began to grow bright.

Royal was still trying to be cheerful. "Well, it's a good day for it."

"I don't see what difference that makes!" Drake grumbled. "I'd just as soon have a bad day to get shot as a good one."

"I sure wish I had my liver pills," Rosie complained.

As the light grew, the squad joined the rest of the company and was put into marching order. They advanced with muskets loaded, and once Lieutenant Logan said, "Keep your bayonets handy in case we have to make a bayonet charge!"

The sun rose, and the birds sang in the trees. It is a beautiful day indeed, Royal thought as he marched along, his eyes peeled for signs of enemy skirmishers. *This would be a good day to be plowing back home—or maybe go fishing down at the creek.* He thought of the easy, pleasant years back in Pineville. They all seemed long ago, and the horrors of months and months of brutal warfare had almost wiped the thought of them from his mind. Now memory came back with a rush.

A crash broke the stillness of the morning air. A shell had struck off to his left, uprooting a chestnut tree and turning it upside down.

Almost instantly rifle fire broke out. As always, it sounded to Royal like thousands of tiny sticks being broken. *Snap! Snap! Snap!*

He yelled, "They're over there, lieutenant!"

"I see them!" Lieutenant Logan said. "Move to the right! Don't fire until you get a good shot!"

As the squad moved forward, shells from the enemy artillery began landing. They made ugly blossoms of dirt, tossing clouds of earth high into the air. The smoke from the muzzles of the distant cannons looked ominous and black. Royal's mouth was dry, and he was already thirsty. Down the line from him, a private gasped, clutched his stomach, and fell.

"Can't stop for him!" Lieutenant Logan said. "Keep going forward! We can't ever stop, or they'll pin us down!"

As Royal moved on, he imagined an evil face painted on each shell. When they exploded, even the sound was like demonic laughter screaming across the sky. More men were falling now, some silently, others crying out for their mothers.

Finally the lieutenant shouted, "Take cover! We can't stand this fire! I'll send for reinforcements!"

The men fell behind whatever shelter was available. Royal gratefully found an old tree and dropped alongside Walter Beddows. The two men loaded and fired as rapidly as possible. Smoke quickly beclouded the area in front of them, but he could still see fleeting forms of the gray-clad enemy moving back and forth through the haze.

"Can't stand much of this!" Walter gasped. He took a swallow of water from his canteen. "I saw Corporal Dobson go down back there. Shot right through the head."

"We're losing too many men," Royal said. "Attacking was a mistake. They're too strong up there."

"How do they expect us to charge against in-place guns?" Drake complained. He rammed a slug home, primed his muzzle, looked around his tree, aimed, and fired, then began rapidly loading again. "They can blast away with those cannons and kill us all! Where's our artillery support?"

"Don't know," Rosie said.

Royal noticed that Rosie was firing as rapidly as he could, apparently having forgotten his imaginary illnesses.

Then Lieutenant Logan came stumbling down the line. "Retreat!" he yelled. "Retreat! Carry the wounded if you can. Don't run! Go back a few yards, stop, fire! Make it an orderly retreat, and we'll be all right!"

Royal looked around at his squad. "All right!" he called. "All of you go on back! I'll cover your retreat!"

Walter placed a wounded private on his shoulders, then said, "Don't wait too long, Royal. I'd hate to see you wind up in a prison camp."

"I'll be all right. Get that soldier to the doctor."

Royal retreated more slowly. He saw that the Confederates were pursuing but with caution. And then he was suddenly surprised to see Drake beside him. "What are you doing still here, Drake?"

Drake's mouth was black from gunpowder where he had bitten the cartridges. He pounded a minié ball down into his musket muzzle and grinned. "Somebody's got to take care of you, sergeant."

A wave of warmth came over Royal. He and Drake had had their troubles, but now, in the heat of battle, the two were forged as one. "I appreciate it," he said, "but now let's get out of—"

"What is it?" Drake said.

"Look, there's one of our fellas over there. I think it's Hotchkiss."

"Wait a minute!" Drake said. "You can't go after him. They'll get you sure, Royal."

"Maybe the smoke's thick enough. You cover me. I'll get Hotchkiss. It won't take but a minute."

Before Drake could argue any longer, Royal leaped to his feet and ran, leaving his rifle, crouching low. From time to time he heard the whine of a minié ball. *An ugly sound,* he thought. Some balls slammed into trees, and he knew that if one hit him, he was a dead man. But then he reached the wounded soldier, who was struggling to get up.

"Sergeant!" Hotchkiss said. He was a young, fair-haired boy. Royal knew he was only seventeen.

"I've got you, Dale. I'll get you out of here."

Royal bent over, thankful for his strength. He pulled Hotchkiss to a sitting position, then positioned him over his shoulder and straightened up. "Now we'll be—"

"Hold it right there, blue belly!"

Royal froze. A Confederate had suddenly materialized out of the smoke. His musket was leveled at his shoulder, and the muzzle looked as big as a cannon.

They've got me! He's going to kill me! Royal thought. He tried to think of a way to escape. He had no musket. But in any case, there was no chance to pick up a weapon—the Rebel's musket was pointed directly at his heart. The soldier's intense, dark brown eyes could be seen blazing under his forage cap.

Royal waited for the explosion and then the blackness that would follow—but they did not come.

The Confederate lowered his rifle slightly. "Hold your head up, blue belly!" he commanded.

Royal obeyed. The smoke was thick, but as the Confederate advanced, suddenly a shock ran through Royal. He knew this man! "Calvin!" he exclaimed. "Is that *you?*"

The Confederate stopped and let his musket droop still lower. "I reckon it is. Didn't expect to see you here, Royal."

The Rebel soldier—Calvin Ramsey—had grown up in a town neighboring Pineville. They had never been close friends but had met at horse races and barn dances and cabin raisings. Once they had been together in a group that made a three-day fishing trip. They had liked each other.

Now, the fortunes of war had brought them face to face.

"I didn't expect to see you either, Calvin."

"I reckon you didn't."

Silence fell as the two men, one in blue and one in gray, stared at each other.

Royal could do nothing but stand waiting, the burden of the wounded man on his back. He said, "I guess you've got me, Calvin. What are you gonna do with me?"

Calvin Ramsey was silent for a moment longer, then sighed. "I almost shot you. Then I thought I'd take you back as a prisoner. But now that I see it's you, Royal—well, I reckon one more blue belly against us ain't gonna make much difference. Go on! Git!"

Royal could not believe his ears. "You mean you're letting me go?"

38

"I think it's all over anyway. We can't win. You and me, we're both Kentucky boys. After the war, maybe you'll think more kindly of the South. Now, git!"

Royal swallowed hard. "Thanks, Calvin. I'll always remember this. Be careful and live out this war. Someday," he said, "we'll go fishing on Eleven Point River again."

Calvin smiled briefly. "I hope that's right. Now, you better git, Royal."

As Royal carried Dale Hotchkiss back toward the Federal lines, his mind was swimming. Then all of a sudden he was aware that Drake stood in front of him.

"Who *was* that? Why'd he let you go?" Drake yelled. "What happened?"

Royal looked back to where Calvin Ramsey had disappeared into the battle smoke. He thought for a while, then turned and said with a slow smile, "What happened, Drake? I guess you might say it was a miracle."

Drake stared at him, clearly not understanding. He too looked into the smoke and said, "I reckon it *was* kind of a miracle, wasn't it?"

"I'd call it so," Royal said. "Now, let's get Dale to the hospital."

4

Drake Takes a Prisoner

The decision to relieve Gen. Joseph E. Johnston of command was due to his having retreated without making a serious effort to stop the Union troops. The man appointed to replace him was Gen. John B. Hood. The men and officers of the Confederate army knew that Hood was an aggressive fighter. He had lost an arm at Gettysburg and a leg at Chickamauga and was admired by all for his courage and loyalty to the Confederacy. But he also was impulsive and apt to lead whole armies to disaster. To a man, the soldiers of his army questioned his judgment.

Royal Carter talked about the Southern generals as the Federal troops waited outside Atlanta. The squad was eating stew made from jackrabbits that Ira Pickens had snared, and from time to time they listened to the guns that were clearly audible in the action closer to the city.

"I'll tell you one man that's glad General Hood will be commanding the Rebels," Royal said.

"Who's that?" Rosie asked, idly smelling the stew.

"General Sherman, that's who. He knew what Johnston could do, and he knows that Hood is different. He knows he can make Hood come out and fight, and then we can whip the Rebels."

Drake Bedford sat off to himself, closer to Rosie than any of the others. He had said practically nothing to anyone since his humiliating punishment and had once remarked to Rosie, "I think I'll just skedaddle back to Tennessee."

"Well, if you want to get hung or shot, I guess that's as good a way as any," Rosie told him. "You know what Sherman would do to any man deserting."

Drake, for all his anger, knew that Rosie spoke the truth. And now he sat listening and saying nothing. He was thinking, *I'd like to get away from here and go court Lori, but there's no chance of that.*

After a while, Captain Salter came by. He was cheerful. "We'll be moving in tomorrow to take the city. I think it's about ready to fall. You fellas will get to be in the assault troops."

"Hey! Tomorrow's September the second, ain't it?" Ira asked.

"That's right," the captain said. "What about it?"

"It's my birthday! I'll be nineteen years old on the day we take Atlanta. Now when we celebrate that, I'll let folks celebrate the takin' of Atlanta and my birthday all together at once."

The next morning some cannons were still pummeling the city when Company A made its charge. They met little resistance except for a few civilians who took potshots at the Union soldiers as they entered the city limits. General Hood had already withdrawn his forces, and there was little to do but go in and assume charge.

Drake was positioned on the far right of the advancing line. The city was smoking from the constant pounding it had taken, and he saw that many buildings were already burned. When the troops came to a large, burned-out factory, he moved off farther to his right and soon found himself alone.

41

He was aware that there could be random shots, and the officers had warned the men that they would have to be careful about diehards who would shoot anything that moved wearing a blue uniform.

Drake carried his loaded musket protectively in front of him. His eyes searched the area carefully as he rounded the corner of the factory. Seeing no one, he advanced slowly, nerves on edge. He passed an alleyway between the charred factory and another building, glanced into it, saw nothing in the dark crevice. He continued on.

However, he had not gone more than three or four steps when he heard a sound behind him. Whirling, he saw a form, a man wearing a dark brown coat and a black slouch hat pulled low over his eyes. The man was also carrying a musket, which he appeared to be raising.

Drake threw up his rifle and in one motion lined up on the man and pulled the trigger.

Nothing!

Misfire. Drake dropped the musket and threw himself into the man. He felt the satisfying impact, saw the rifle go cartwheeling through the air, and heard the man expel his breath in a violent grunt as he was driven to the ground.

Drake grabbed the man by the lapels and jerked him to his feet. He saw a pair of black eyes staring out at him, and he noted quickly that his prisoner was very young.

"Tryin' to shoot me in the back, were you?"

"Didn't mean to shoot nobody." The voice was quiet, and there was no fear in the dark eyes that gazed back at him. "You didn't have to knock me down like that."

"You had a rifle, and you were behind me. What are you doin' here with a gun if you didn't mean to shoot me?"

"I'm lost, that's what."

"A likely story!" Drake jeered. He looked at the youth, who was no more than five seven and wore what appeared to be a cast-off set of clothes—faded blue trousers, a checkered shirt, and a light coat, buttoned despite the heat. The hat was drawn down so far over the fellow's eyes that it almost covered his ears. It looked like a hat that had belonged to a much larger man. The shoes, he saw, were large too, and the sole of one was tied on with a leather thong.

"What are you goin' to do with me?"

Drake was uncertain. He looked around for any officers or men of Company A but saw no one. "Come with me," he said. "I'll turn you over to the officers. They can decide what to do with you."

"I'll get my rifle gun."

"Never mind! *I'll* get your gun," Drake retorted. He picked up the rifle and looked at it. It was an old gun, well-worn. "Where'd you get this rifle, fella?"

"Belonged to my pa!"

"Where's your pa?"

The black eyes dropped for a moment as the youngster looked down at his feet. "He's dead now. Got killed two days ago. Shell fell on him."

Drake hesitated. He had seen the pain that came into the boy's dark eyes at the mention of his father, and he wanted to say he was sorry. But this, after all, was the enemy, and Drake was still convinced that the young fellow had tried to shoot him in the back. "I can't let you go. I'll have to turn you over to the officers. They'll make the decision. Come on."

He waited, and when the boy moved with him, he started back the way he had come.

Back at the Union camp, Drake found that some of his squad had already returned. Major Bates was just coming out of his tent. Seeing no other officers, Drake walked up to him and said, "Major, sir, this here civilian tried to shoot me. I took his rifle away from him, but I was afraid to turn him loose."

A small crowd began to gather, and Major Bates, a tall man with a powerful voice, looked at the prisoner with some disdain. "We're not supposed to be fightin' civilians!"

"I didn't know what else to do with him, major. It's up to you."

Major Bates hesitated. Some civilians had indeed been shooting at the troops, and this might be one of them. "We'll just hold him here until we get the city secured. Where you from?" he asked the prisoner.

"Used to be from Macon, but I ain't from nowhere now!"

Major Bates seemed taken aback. "What do you mean, you're not from anywhere?"

"I mean me and Pa came here a spell back, and then you Yankees come and surrounded the city. And day before yesterday my pa got killed when a cannonball fell on him."

Major Bates stared hard at the young face. "I'm sorry about your father. You have any other relatives?"

"No, it was just me and Pa—now I guess there's just me."

"Well, you can't go running around the city. One of our men's liable to shoot you if they see you sneakin' around with a rifle."

"I don't know where else to go! Pa sold the farm when we left from Macon, and now there ain't nothin' to go back to there."

Major Bates glanced around at the soldiers and saw Royal. "Sergeant," he said, "take care of this young fella. Keep him close until the city is secured, then you can let him go."

"Yes, sir!"

Major Bates turned and left.

Royal came forward and said reassuringly to the boy. "You'll be all right." Then he looked at Drake. "I guess he's your prisoner, Drake, so you can watch out for him."

"I ain't baby-sittin' no Reb prisoners!" Drake said. But he said it carefully, for he was still keenly aware of having ridden the wooden horse.

"I don't need nobody to take care of me!" the prisoner exclaimed.

Drake turned on him with some irritation. "Well, you can't take care of yourself! I'da shot you back there, only my rifle misfired." He still could not see the boy's face very well. "Take off that blasted hat so I can see what you look like!"

Drake jerked the hat off the prisoner's head, and a wealth of curly brown hair cascaded down over the shoulders of what was clearly a young woman.

A gasp went around the group of soldiers that had gathered to watch the scene.

"By george!" Rosie said. "That there's a *girl* prisoner you got there, Drake!"

"Boy, you're some soldier, ain't you, Drake?" Walter Beddows said. "Caught that young lady all by yourself, did you?"

45

The men laughed. Drake flushed and felt anger rising. He threw down the hat. The laughter grew, and his face grew hotter.

Royal said, "You fellas clear out of here. Drake, you come with me—and you too. What's your name?"

The girl picked up the hat. "Charlie."

Royal stared at her. "That's no name for a girl! What's your real name?"

She twisted the hat around in her hands. She appeared as embarrassed by the laughter of the soldiers as Drake was. She almost whispered, "My real name is Charlene, but Pa always just called me Charlie."

"Well, come on, Miss Charlene," Royal said. He led Charlie off to the mess tent, where he sat her down. "Now, tell me where you're from and what you're doing here in Atlanta."

"My name's Charlene Satterfield. Me and Pa come here after we sold the farm, and Pa thought he'd go into business here. He always wanted to be a saddle maker. Then the Yankees come, and we couldn't get out." Her eyes filled with tears. Her voice faltered. "And then Pa got kilt."

"Well, I'm real sorry about that, Miss Charlene. How old are you?"

"Almost eighteen."

"You got any relatives or friends in Atlanta?"

"No, there was just me and Pa."

Drake stood by, listening with chagrin.

Royal turned to him. "Did you really try to shoot her, Drake?" he asked caustically.

"I didn't *know* it was a girl. She had a rifle in her hand, and she come up behind me . . ." Drake suspected his face was still red. He felt a surge of shame when he considered that he might have shot

46

a girl. "She didn't have no business comin' out of that alley behind me," he said roughly.

"I didn't even know you was there," Charlie said. She was watching Drake, studying his countenance. "What's *your* name, soldier?"

Drake glared at her. "Drake Bedford."

The girl's lips turned up. "My, ain't that purty! Drake. I ain't never known no boy named Drake."

Royal watched this and then said, "Drake, I've got something to tell you. We've got to do something with this young lady."

"Well, *I* don't know what to do with her. I didn't join the army to take care of stray girls!"

For a moment Royal hesitated, then said, "There's something I haven't told you yet. I got a letter from Lori."

Instantly Drake turned his eyes toward Royal.

"She's here in Atlanta."

"What's she doin' *here?*"

"She's got an aunt here. Her father's sister, and she's real old and needed help." Taking a slip out of his inner pocket, Royal handed it over. "As you can see, she just wanted to let me know that she was here. And she says to tell you too."

"Why didn't she write to me?" Drake said sullenly.

"I guess she thought a sergeant would get a letter quicker than a private."

Drake studied the letter. "I guess you're planning to go callin' on her."

Royal probably had planned doing exactly that, but he shook his head. "I can't leave camp. The lieutenant's gone, and I can't get away till he gets back." He looked again at their prisoner. "I'll tell you what. I think Miss Lori would be glad to look out for you until things settle down a bit here."

"Who is this Miss Lori?" the girl asked with interest. Her eyes still had not left Drake's face, but she listened as Royal explained.

"She's a young lady from Tennessee. She's come down, as you heard me say, to be with her elderly aunt. I expect you could stay with her. She says her aunt's got a big house. I think they could probably find room until you decide on what to do."

"I don't know. I don't know what to do."

There was a plaintive quality to the girl's voice. She seemed sturdy enough, but the loss of her father had no doubt shaken her. And now she stood there in her oversized, worn clothes, a pathetic figure.

Royal said, "Drake, Lori tells in this letter where her aunt's house is, so you take Miss Charlene over there and ask Lori if she'll keep her until she can decide what to do."

Suspiciously Drake said, "Why are you lettin' *me* go see Lori?"

"Because I can't leave here, like I told you!" Royal snapped. "Will that be all right with you, Miss Charlene?"

"I reckon so. You'll be takin' me, will you, Mr. Drake?"

"I guess I will. Come on, then."

As they left camp, Drake had to endure some more teasing. "If you capture any more girls, bring some back for us!" Ira Pickens called out.

His face burning, Drake stomped off, conscious that the girl was staying close to his side. He did not look at her for a long time but simply walked straight forward.

"Do you know where we're goin', Mr. Drake?" she asked.

48

"The letter says that Miss Lori's aunt lives right down the street from the city hall. That ought not be too hard to find."

Silence ran on as the two made their way back into town and through the blasted streets of Atlanta. People were beginning to move about, and Charlie kept close.

Suddenly he thought of something, and he turned and looked down at her. "You got stuff? Where are your things?"

"Back in that alley. I slept there last night."

"Then why didn't you—what about your pa? Is he . . . is he buried?"

The girl's eyes turned to him, and her lip trembled. She looked fragile despite her height. "Yep, the preacher at the Baptist church, he buried Pa. He said some good words over him too."

"All right. We'll have to go back to that alley and get your things."

They found the alleyway. Charlie darted inside and came out with a bedroll and a large canvas bag, evidently stuffed full.

"Give me the bag," Drake said with irritation and picked it up. "Let's go find Lori and get you a place to stay."

Lori Jenkins, a small girl with a wealth of auburn hair, brown eyes, and an oval face, looked surprised to see Drake at her door. "Why, Drake," she said, "I didn't expect to see you so soon."

"Royal showed me your letter," he said. "Are you all right?"

"Yes, of course, I'm all right. And you're not hurt? Neither you nor Royal?"

"No, we're both all right."

She glanced at Drake's companion and waited for an introduction.

"This here's—Charlie. Well, her real name's Charlene," Drake mumbled. He chewed his lip. "She's in quite a bind, Lori. She doesn't have any place to stay, and her father got killed recently."

Instantly Lori said, "Come in, Charlene." She took the girl's arm and drew her inside. "I'm so sorry about your father."

Charlie pulled her hat off, and the thick, springy curls fell around her shoulders again. She raked a hand through them, trying to create some order, but it was hopeless. They framed her face in a halo as she studied the smaller girl with her large, dark eyes. "I don't want to put you out," she said.

"We've plenty of room here. My aunt is Mrs. Holcomb. She's very old and needs care. Maybe you can help me take care of her."

"I could do that. I can keep house a little bit—and maybe cook some."

"Fine," Lori said. "Now that's settled. Both of you come into the kitchen and sit down. I've got some ham cooked, and we can all have lunch together."

As they ate, Charlie kept her eyes fixed mostly on Drake. From time to time she would examine the pretty face of the girl who sat across from her, but she said little or nothing.

Finally Drake got up to return to camp. "Well, Charlie," he said, "I'm glad I didn't shoot you."

"I'm proud you didn't, Mr. Drake."

"I'll be seeing you later." Drake turned to Lori then. "Don't know how long we'll be here. Can I come back and call on you?"

"Of course you can, Drake. That's why I sent the note."

"I reckon Royal will be wantin' to come too."

"He's very welcome."

Drake did not find that an attractive thought.

As soon as the door closed, Charlie turned to Lori. "He's a fine-lookin' fella, ain't he, now?"

"Yes, Drake's very nice-looking."

"Is he married up with anybody?"

Lori smiled slightly and shook her head. "No, he's not."

"Is he spoken for?"

"I don't think he is."

Charlie leaned back in her chair, picked up a bit of ham, and chewed it thoughtfully. "He's a big fella. I always did think big fellas were nice."

"Did you now?"

"Yep, I sure did."

Lori appraised the girl and the awkward clothes that scarcely fit anywhere. "What about yourself, Charlie? Have you been to school?"

"Pa taught me my letters. Mostly I been huntin' and fishin'. I had two sisters. They're both married up now, off in Louisiana."

"You'll want to go stay with them, I suppose?"

"No, don't reckon I will." Charlie picked up her glass of tea and sipped it with satisfaction. Then she murmured dreamily, "He sure is a fine-lookin' fella, Mr. Drake. Ain't he, now?"

5
Colonel Majors and His Nurse

Col. Nelson Majors looked up from where he sat in a padded chair and smiled. "My favorite nurse coming with my favorite breakfast."

Eileen Fremont was a small woman with red hair and green eyes and was wearing a blue-and-white apron over a dark blue dress. She had undertaken the care of the colonel's three-year-old daughter and then, when the colonel was wounded, had gotten him out of the military hospital, where care was sometimes terrible, to care for him at home. She had grown very fond of her patient. They planned to marry soon.

"I don't know what your favorite breakfast is. Everything I bring, you gobble down like a bear."

"You shouldn't be such a good cook. Now, sit down and talk to me while I eat."

"I have housework to do."

"I'm your patient. I'm more important than any housework." He reached out and took Eileen's wrist as she set down the tray on the table next to him. "After all, I'm a sick man. You need to humor me a little bit."

Eileen sat. She could not resist smiling back at the tall soldier. Nelson Majors was more than six feet, with very black hair and intense hazel eyes. He had a neat mustache and was close shaven.

"Now then, let's see what we have here," he said as he looked at the tray. "It looks like eggs, grits, biscuits, and sawmill gravy. Is that all I get?" he asked mischievously.

Eileen laughed aloud. "You're going to be fat as a suckling pig if you keep on eating, Nelson." She watched him pour coffee out of a china pot into a thick mug. "But I like to see a man enjoy his food. I've missed having someone to cook for."

The colonel looked up quickly, swallowed a bite of biscuit soaked with gravy, and said, "It does get lonesome sometimes, doesn't it?"

Eileen had lost her husband at Shiloh and shortly after that her two-year-old daughter. She smoothed her hair over the back of her head and nodded. "It's good you have Tom and Jeff."

"I won't have them long. They'll get married and be gone. That's what young men do."

"Fortunately you'll still have Esther. She's only three. She's going to take a lot of raising."

"And I'm an old man to be raising a little girl," he said thoughtfully. He took a bite of grits. "These are good, Eileen. You're a fine cook."

"Anybody can cook breakfast. How can you mess up eggs and grits?" She leaned back in the chair and folded her hands. As Nelson continued to eat, she said, "Esther's outside with Leah. I never saw a child who likes to dig in the dirt so much—except boys."

"I guess she takes after me," he murmured. Then he added, "She looks like her mother, though. Same blonde hair and blue eyes."

He had lost his wife at the birth of this child. Eileen knew he was uncertain how he would do at raising a small daughter—and even more uncertain because of the battles that lay ahead.

"I just don't know what would happen to Esther if anything happened to me in battle," he said.

"Tom and Jeff would take care of her." Even as she said this, however, Eileen knew that this was not the answer. Both of his sons were also in the army and were subject to the dangers of the war. She smoothed her apron over her lap and said, "The war is almost over. It can't go on much longer, can it?"

"No, I don't think it can. The South has just worn itself out. The best of its young men went at the first call, and now we're down to just a thin line." He looked out the window thoughtfully, then suddenly turned to her. "Eileen, would you take care of Esther —if anything happens to me before we marry?"

"But Nelson, don't you have family who would want—"

"No, I didn't have any brothers or sisters. My wife had one sister, but she's far away in the North now. There's really no one."

Eileen hesitated. "That's a large thing to promise —to take over a baby. Not that I wouldn't love to. I still miss my own little girl." Tears came to her eyes, and she dashed them away quickly. "Of course I will, Nelson. If that's what you want—but nothing's going to happen to you. We'll just pray you through until this war is over."

"I'll agree with that." He leaned back after finishing his breakfast and sighed with satisfaction. "Almost hate to get well," he said. "Here I am being waited on hand and foot by a handsome woman, getting good food, treated like a baby. Not like it'll be when I go back to the trenches at Petersburg."

Eileen did not answer. She was thinking of the dangers that lay ahead for this tall man who had come to mean so much to her. She got up to take the tray. "Do you want anything else?"

"No, this is fine."

She touched a lock of his glossy, black hair. "You're getting shaggy. I'll have to give you another haircut."

The colonel took her hand, and before she could move he kissed it and said huskily, "Thanks for all you've done for the Majors family. For Esther and for me."

"Come on in, Jeff."

Leah stepped back from the doorway to let him in. Jeff was wearing his oldest uniform, which was far gone.

"How's Pa today?"

"You'll have to ask his nurse. Eileen's just about taken over."

Jeff frowned. For a long time he had been jealous of Mrs. Fremont. He had loved his mother deeply and resented the idea of his father's being interested in another woman. Somehow it had seemed disloyal to him. He still occasionally felt a little strange at the idea. "I thought Tom would be here."

"I *am* here!" Tom walked in from the kitchen, a piece of pie balanced on one hand. He limped slightly, and the wooden leg that replaced the real one that he'd lost at Gettysburg made an uncertain cadence on the floor. "What are you doing here, Jeff?"

"I came looking for something to eat. We're about to run shy in camp. What kind of pie is that?"

"It's apple."

"My favorite kind!"

"I'm glad to hear it. This is the last piece," Tom said and winked at Leah.

Jeff groaned. "You didn't eat it *all!*"

"Don't let him tease you, Jeff," Leah said. "I made two. We'll have some after while."

"How's Pa?" Jeff asked his brother.

"Real good." Tom licked his hand and took another bite of pie. "Somehow pie always tastes better if you eat it off your hand. A fork kind of spoils the taste."

Leah said, "I'll get you a piece, Jeff, and maybe we have some sassafras tea."

"That'd be good." He waited until she was gone and then sat down, looking at his brother. "You think Pa will be able to get back into the fight pretty soon?"

"You know Pa. He'll get back as quick as he can. As a matter of fact, I wish he'd stay out of the whole thing."

"It looks pretty grim, Tom. I don't know how much longer we can keep those Yankees out. We're spread real thin."

"And our fellows aren't doing much better out west of here. Hood's left Atlanta now, so the word is. But Sherman will catch up with him. Johnston should have stayed in command."

"Well, he wasn't doin' anything much to stop General Sherman!" Jeff protested.

"Sherman's got too many men. All Hood will do is make some kind of a crazy charge and lose half the army." Tom finished his pie and wiped his hands with a handkerchief. "I'm going outside and split some wood. After you get through with your pie, you can come out and help me with the buck-sawing."

"All right, Tom."

Jeff met Leah coming out of the kitchen with his pie. "I can just eat it out here in the kitchen," he said. "It'll save you bringin' me another piece." He grinned at her, took the plate and fork, and said, "Tom, he's a glutton. He gobbles pie down like a pig. Now me, I got taste." He took a small bite, put it in his mouth, then lifted his eyes toward the ceiling with appreciation. "Now, that is pie!"

Leah smiled. "Do you really like it?"

"I never saw an apple pie I didn't like—especially yours."

They sat at the kitchen table, talking and laughing, until finally Jeff said, "Go take off that dress and put your old overalls on. It's time to go fishin'."

"Why, Jeff, you didn't say anything about us going fishing."

"I thought you knew," he said in surprise.

"I can't go with you, Jeff."

"Why not?"

"Because—I've got somebody coming."

Jeff stared at her. He suddenly realized she was wearing her silk Sunday dress. It was a peach color and old, but she still looked good in it. "What do you mean, somebody's coming?"

Leah hesitated, then smiled roguishly. "Cecil is coming by."

"Cecil Taylor? Why's *he* coming here?"

Leah's eyes gleamed. "He's coming to see me!"

"Why's he coming to see you?"

"Does it come as a complete shock to you, Jeff," she asked demurely, "that a young man would like to come and spend some time with me?"

He felt foolish. "Well . . ." He floundered for a time. "Well, of course not, but how does he have time to come out here and see you?"

"How do you have time?" she asked quickly.

Jeff saw that he was trapped and somehow felt put out. "Well, I planned to go fishing with you . . ."

"We can do that tomorrow—unless Cecil comes back."

"Oh, I'm good enough to go fishing with if there's nothing better to do."

Moving around the table to where Jeff now stood rigidly, she put a hand on his arm and looked up into his face. She said sweetly, "I'm sorry, Jeff. I didn't mean to say it like that. You know how much I like to go fishing with you. I always have. But Cecil wanted to come over, and he gets lonesome sometimes."

"Well, I get lonesome too."

"Do you, Jeff?"

"Of course I do. Do you think I like being in trenches with those dirty, smelly soldiers? I'd much rather be here with you."

"I guess *that's* a left-handed compliment." But Leah again smiled. "You like me better than dirty, smelly soldiers."

Jeff felt he was in over his head. "I can't say anything right today," he said finally. "So what are you two going to do?"

"Oh, I don't know. I thought we would look at some picture albums. Maybe we'll sing some. Cecil has a beautiful singing voice. And I need to give him some more dancing lessons. He's not very good at dancing, but he's getting better."

At that moment, a knock sounded on the door, and Leah said, "That must be Cecil now. He'll be glad to see you."

As it happened, Cecil seemed not particularly happy to see Jeff. And Jeff was rather grumpy as he said, "Hello, Cecil."

"Well, hello, Jeff. I didn't know you'd be here."

"I didn't know you'd be here either!" He saw that Cecil had on his best uniform, and he asked rather wickedly, "Are you going to another ball?"

"No, I just came to call on Leah."

She said, "Why don't both of you come into the sitting room? Jeff, you've already seen all the pictures, but Cecil would like to see them."

Jeff said stubbornly, "No, I'm going fishing."

He left the house, slamming the door slightly harder than was necessary.

Immediately he heard his father's voice. "Jeff, come here!"

Jeff lifted his head and saw the colonel leaning out a window. He stomped over to him and said, "What is it, Pa?"

"Where you going?"

"I'm going to get a pole and go fishing."

"Why don't you take Leah with you?"

"I came to do that, but instead Cecil Taylor came to call on her."

Nelson grinned. "You better watch out. That young fellow's gonna to beat your time."

Jeff flushed. "Who needs an old girl anyway?"

Tom leaned over the windowsill beside his father and studied Jeff. "I reckon most of us do."

Jeff and his father both glanced at Tom. Jeff knew his brother was thinking of Sarah, Leah's older sister. Tom had been deeply in love with Sarah before

59

the war. Now Tom's face was sad, and his thoughts seemed to be a million miles away.

"I guess most of us do need a lady to make our lives bright," their father said.

Jeff stared at the colonel. He knew that the object of *his* thoughts was Eileen Fremont.

"I'm going fishing!" Jeff said. He turned around and went toward the barn.

From his window Colonel Majors watched Jeff come out of the barn with a pole over his shoulder and a can of worms dangling from one hand. Then he turned to Tom.

"I guess you think about Sarah a lot."

"Yes, I do, Pa. I miss her more than I can say."

"I know about that. It's the same way I miss your mother."

When Eileen came into the room, the men were playing checkers.

Tom got up in disgust. "I can't beat you at this game!"

"You're too impulsive. You've got to think out your moves," Nelson said.

"I'm going out to chop more wood. It's more fun than getting beat at checkers."

After Tom left, Eileen sat down at Nelson's bidding, and they began another checkers game. She was not very good, and Nelson was an excellent player. Nevertheless, he used the game as an excuse to keep her in his room.

Eventually they began talking about the boys, and Nelson laid out their problems. His brow furrowed as he talked of Tom's love for Sarah Carter and his recurring uncertainty about marrying her because he had lost a leg. "And now Jeff's growing up," he added, "and you know how hard it is to raise a young boy. I was hard to raise myself."

Eileen smiled. "They're both fine boys," she said. "You have a fine family, Nelson, and they're all going to turn out well."

6

Charlie Makes a Decision

The battle for Atlanta had been terrible. Many buildings were destroyed, and their gutted skeletons pointed like ghostly fingers to the sky. Many citizens had lost their homes. The struggle to rebuild the city had begun. Now, however, Atlanta was a Yankee city rather than one that had been the pride of the Confederacy.

Mrs. Grace Holcomb, the aunt of Lori Jenkins, was a frail, silver-haired lady in her late eighties. Although she had many friends from a lifelong residency in Atlanta, she was totally without family there.

Her eyes lit up with gratitude as Lori put her breakfast tray in place. "Lori, I don't know what I would have done," she said, and her hands trembled as she reached out to pat Lori's arm. "You were like an angel from heaven when you suddenly appeared," she added, smiling up at her.

Lori had heard that her aunt had been a beautiful woman in her youth, and traces of that beauty remained. She returned Mrs. Holcomb's smile and poured a cup of tea into a dainty china cup. "I'm just glad I could come, Aunt Grace. It's good to visit with you and hear the stories of the family."

She sat down beside the elderly woman and talked cheerfully, studying the old lady's face. *She doesn't look well*, Lori thought. *Every day she seems to get a little weaker, but she never is discouraged. She's really a wonderful woman.*

"Have you heard from your parents, Lori?"

"Oh, yes. They say the Yankees are still holding Tennessee. I suppose there's no hope for the Confederacy there."

Aunt Grace sighed. "Such a terrible war. I wish it had never happened. What will happen to the poor South?"

Lori at one time would have said quickly that the South had not lost the war. Now, however, the news was so bad that she no longer felt that way. Sherman was pursuing General Hood's troops across Tennessee, and it was just a matter of time before the huge Union Army won over the smaller Confederate force.

"I don't think it can last much longer, Aunt Grace," she said. "Soon it will all be over, and life can go on again."

Grace Holcomb's eyes dimmed as she looked over at her niece. "I hope all goes well for you, Lori." She nibbled at her toast and then asked, "What about these two young men that you keep talking about? Royal and Drake. Tell me some more about them."

Lori's cheeks grew warm, and she laughed slightly. "Oh, you know how it is, Aunt Grace."

"It's been a long time since I was a girl. But I still remember two boys that got into a fight over me out in the schoolyard." She smiled gently. "I wonder where they are now. Probably in their graves, both of them. I think of them still. Have they fought over you yet, these two young men?"

"Oh, yes, but I'm hoping they'll stop such foolishness."

The two women talked while Mrs. Holcomb finished her breakfast.

"This was so good, Lori. I don't know how we're going to manage for food in the future. I don't have very much money left."

"Oh, Daddy gave me plenty of money." Lori grinned, adding, "It's all in Confederate money. I don't know if the Yankees will let us use it or not. And that reminds me—I've got to go out and get some groceries."

"From what I hear from the ladies that come and visit, most of the shops are pretty bare, and it's still dangerous for a young woman to be out."

"Royal's coming by. He'll escort me down to see what we can find. Now, I won't be leaving you alone. Charlie will be here."

"Charlie. What an odd name for a young woman." Mrs. Holcomb shook her head in disbelief. "I don't know why she persists in calling herself that."

"I expect that's just what she likes to be called. I tried to call her Charlene a few times, and she seemed very uncomfortable with it. I'll have her check on you while Royal and I are getting the groceries."

When Royal appeared at the door, he was met by Charlie, wearing the same outfit he had seen on her the day she was captured. "Hello, Charlie!" he greeted her. "Is Lori here?"

"Yep! She's upstairs redd'n up. She sure is lookin' forward to goin' with you."

Charlie's speech had a country flavor to it. Her cheeks were pink, and there was a cheerfulness about her that pleased Royal. Most girls he knew who had

had Charlie's troubles would not have handled them so well.

Lori came in at that moment, wearing a light green dress and a straw hat with a flower pinned to the top. "I'm ready, Royal."

The two started for the door, and Lori remarked as she went out, "Charlie, would you check on Aunt Grace? Be sure that she has all she needs?"

"Sure, I'll do that," Charlie agreed.

Lori's aunt was sitting up in bed reading the Bible that was propped on her lap when Charlie came in.

"Got some lemonade for you, Miss Grace. Not cold, 'cause we ain't got no ice, but thought you might like it."

Mrs. Holcomb put aside the Bible and smiled at the tall girl. "Why, thank you, Charlene." As she took the glass, she saw that the use of Charlie's proper name had somehow embarrassed her. Sipping the lemonade, she studied the girl. The old woman's sharp eyes went over the crisp, curly, brown hair and the clear, large, dark eyes. The overalls she wore were clean, though patched and faded. She noted that the girl had a fine figure, though disguised by her outlandish garb.

"This is very good, Charlene. Did you make some for yourself?"

"Oh, no. I usually drink coffee. Of course, lately we've been trying to make coffee out of burnt acorns. Don't care for that too much."

"Did you lose all of your possessions in the attack, Charlene?"

"Oh, no. I brought 'em. They're in the room down the hall where Miss Lori put me."

"Well . . . didn't you have any dresses? I notice you keep on wearing the same overalls every day."

"Oh, I've got a dress, but I don't care to wear 'em much. Lots easier to get around in overalls than it is in dresses."

Until now, Mrs. Holcomb had spoken only briefly with the young woman. "Tell me about yourself, Charlene," she said, doggedly refusing to use what she considered the ugly name of Charlie. "Tell me about your family. You have brothers and sisters?"

"Had two sisters, but they moved off. Me and Pa handled the farm, and they did the cookin' and the housework when they was home. They was real little, you see, Miss Grace, and I was big and strong." She nodded proudly. "I can plow as good as most men."

"I'm sure you can," she said. "But didn't you learn how to cook and do housework?"

"Oh, I can cook a steak, I guess. Never did much of the housework though."

Charlie went on describing her life, which sounded appalling to Mrs. Holcomb. *Poor child,* she thought. *She really doesn't know the first thing about keeping house. How will she ever in this world make a man a good wife?* Aloud she said cautiously, "I think it would be nice if you would dress up for supper tonight. You know . . . fix your hair and put on the dress . . ."

"Oh, I don't reckon I'll do that, Miss Grace," Charlie said carelessly. "Lots of work to do around here. The shells took out some of the fencin'. I been puttin' it back. And the well curbing got busted too. I got to lay some new curbstones around that if I can get ahold of some cement."

"Do you know how to do things like that?"

"Oh, yes, ma'am, I do. I done that kind of work all my life. There ain't nothin' around a place that I can't do if I set my mind to it."

Charlie sat sprawled in her chair in a most unladylike position. She really had none of the feminine graces. For all the striking beauty of her face and attractiveness of her figure, she looked more like a pretty young man than a young woman.

Finally she got up, took the glass from Mrs. Holcomb, and said, "Reckon I'll go out and chop some wood. Got to sharpen the ax first, though. It's plumb dull."

After the girl left, Mrs Holcomb said aloud, "How in the world will she ever survive?" Shaking her head, she picked up the Bible and began reading. After a time she thought of Charlene again, and she prayed a quick, simple prayer. "Lord, make a woman out of that girl. She doesn't even know that she's a woman, and she's headed for some hard times if she doesn't learn."

Drake arrived in front of the Holcomb cottage just as the sun was beginning to set. He had come at Lori's invitation, and he wore his good uniform. Knocking, he hoped fervently that he would have Lori to himself tonight. When the door opened, however, it was not Lori but Charlie Satterfield who stood there.

"Why, howdy, Drake!" she said and stuck out her hand out like a man. "Come on in the house."

Rather taken off guard, Drake found his hand grasped firmly. Charlie's handshake, he discovered, was not like a young lady's but was strong and firm. His hand was pumped up and down, and then he was propelled into the house by a quick jerk.

67

"Uh . . . thank you, Charlie," he mumbled. He noted that she was still wearing overalls. She wore a man's white shirt, and the brown hair framing her face was very curly.

"Miss Lori's gettin' herself all cleaned up," she announced. "You know Mrs. Holcomb's got a copper bathtub?"

"No, I didn't know that," Drake said as he followed Charlie, who strode with long, purposeful steps to the sitting room.

"Yep, that's right. I het water for it and filled it up so she could have a good all-over bath." Charlie waved at a red plush chair and waited until Drake had lowered himself into it. Then she turned a smaller chair around and straddled it. "That's right," she said. "It took me about ten trips with a teakettle, but I got it all hetted up. She sure ought to be clean with all that hot water and soap and all that perfume and stuff she uses. Sure is a sight of trouble. Don't see no need of it myself."

Drake studied the girl cautiously. He had not spoken with her except for a brief greeting since he had captured her, and now he asked, "Uh . . . how are you getting along, Charlie?"

"Me? Oh, I'm doin' fine. I'm helpin' around the place here, don't you see? Miss Grace, she ain't feelin' well, and Lori, she has to take lots of care of her. So I chop the wood and milk the cow and do everything that needs doin'. Not much work around here though. Back home we had forty acres. Wasn't nothin' for me to get up and plow from sunup to sundown." She teetered back and forth on the chair. "I sure do miss my mules! Buddy and Bob their names were. Best set of mules in the state of Georgia."

Drake shifted uncomfortably. "Uh . . . have you made any plans . . . about what you're going to do, I mean?"

"Not yet."

"But you'll have to sooner or later, won't you?"

"Guess so, but right now I think I'm just gonna help Miss Lori take care of Miss Grace. Tell me about your soldierin'. Have you ever been shot?"

Drake grinned. "Not yet."

"That's good. A fella that lived down the road from us went off to fight the Yankees, and he came back. He had his ear shot plumb off! Just one of 'em though. Didn't hurt his hearin' none."

Charlie carried the bulk of the conversation until Lori came in. She looked sparkling fresh, and she wore a dress that Drake had not seen before. Getting to his feet, he said, "Hello, Lori. My, you're looking real good tonight."

"Good to see you, Drake. Would you come on up and meet my aunt?"

"I'd be glad to."

Drake accompanied Lori upstairs where he met Mrs. Holcomb. But she seemed weak and was unable to entertain them very long. When they left her room, he said with a frown, "She doesn't look good, Lori."

Lori's face was sad. "She's not doing very well at all. Every day it seems she's a little weaker."

"Do you think she's going to make it?"

"I don't know. She's getting on, and she's had a lot of sickness . . ." She seemed not to want to talk about her aunt. She said, "What do you think of your prisoner?"

Drake grinned rather feebly. "She's as good a fella as I've ever seen. Does she ever wear anything except overalls?"

"Not that I know of. I've tried to get her into a dress. She won't listen."

"Well, she's resourceful enough."

"Oh, she's all that. She chops the wood, milks the cow, feeds the chickens. She does all the things that have to be done outside. She's building a new well wall for us. You ought to see her out there with a trowel, putting those rocks in place."

Drake said, "Well, I didn't come to talk about her. I came to talk about us."

"Come on down to the kitchen, and I'll give you some apple cake that I made," Lori said quickly.

The evening did not go as Drake had planned. Charlie came into the kitchen almost at once and did everything but sit between them. When they went into the parlor, Charlie was there. She did not appear at all aware that she was intruding. Her eyes went from Lori to Drake, and from time to time she would ask questions of one or the other. At other times she simply sat, usually with her eyes fixed upon Drake.

When Drake was leaving to go back to camp in disgust, he said to Lori in one private moment snatched out on the porch, "Can't you get rid of her? She's always right between us!"

"She's lonesome, I think," Lori said.

"Well, I'm lonesome, too," he muttered. "I wanted to see *you*, not some girl who can't make up her mind what she is."

"Good night, Drake. I must go in now."

He stood looking at the door that slowly closed, then angrily turned away. "I can't believe that Charlie!"

Drake marched back to camp, a long walk, and found that more of his squad members had learned about his prisoner. They teased him about her until he grew so angry that they finally refrained.

When Drake saw Royal, he said, "Did *you* tell the fellas about Charlie?"

Royal looked up with surprise. "Just that the girl prisoner was living with Lori and her aunt. Why?"

"I just wanted to know. I won't put up with any ragging about her. You understand me, sergeant?"

"Not from me, Drake. She's a fine girl, though."

Drake shook his head. "That may be, but she sure is a pest!"

7

Worse Than a Chigger

Lori became more and more troubled about her aunt. Mrs. Holcomb was failing swiftly, and finally Lori sent for the doctor.

A tall man with a gray beard, Dr. Smith examined his elderly patient and later told Lori privately, "She's weaker every time I see her. There's only one end to this I'm afraid, Miss Jenkins."

Lori had feared that was the case. "Will she die soon, doctor?"

Dr. Smith chewed his lower lip. "Impossible to say. You'll just have to give her the best care you can. She's a good Christian woman and ready to go."

"Oh, yes. I've never known anybody more ready to meet death than Aunt Grace."

After the doctor left, Lori saw Charlie outside splitting wood. She went to the door and called out, "Charlie, come in. I want to talk to you."

Charlie came inside, her face reddened from exercise. "What is it, Lori?"

"It's about my aunt. She's not doing very well."

"Oh, I'm sorry to hear that. Couldn't the doctor give her some medicine?"

"He didn't think that would help. She's very old, you know, and it's just about her time to go."

Charlie's face fell. "She's been talkin' to me a lot about the Bible. She was real glad to hear I was a Christian."

"I'm glad to hear it too, Charlie."

"Yep, I got saved at a revival meetin' three summers ago. I don't read too good, but I read the Bible all the time."

"Sit down, Charlie. I want to talk to you a while."

"That's good. I want to talk to you too."

They sat at the table, and before Lori could speak, Charlie began. "You know, I been thinkin' a lot about what I want to do. I know you been worried about me, Lori, haven't you?"

"Well . . . you seem so alone, Charlie. No family. I *have* been concerned about you. Have you decided on something?"

"Sure have!" Charlie clasped her hands around her knees and rocked back and forth. It was a boyish gesture, but it was somehow winsome in her. "I reckon I'll get hitched."

For a moment Lori could not understand what she meant, and then the meaning became clear. "You mean . . . get married?"

"Sure, that's what I mean. I'm going to get married."

Lori could not have been more surprised if Charlie had told her she was going to walk on the moon. "But I didn't even know you were thinking of getting married!"

Shrugging her shoulders, Charlie said, "I thought about it once or twice, but back home in Macon it didn't seem to be what I ought to do. There was the farm to take care of, and I had to help Pa with that. But I'm gettin' pretty old now not to be married. Lots of girls get married when they're two or three years younger than I am."

"But who are you going to marry?"

"Oh, I done figured I'd marry up with Drake."

73

Lori was totally speechless. She stared at the girl across from her, who could not have understood the enormity of what she was saying. She realized suddenly that Charlene Satterfield had had none of the upbringing that young women usually had. She said carefully, not wanting to hurt Charlie's feelings, "But Charlie, does Drake know this?"

"Not yet, but I figure to tell him."

Lori cleared her throat. "That's not the way it happens."

"What do you mean, not the way it happens?"

"I mean that young men do the courting, not young women."

"Oh, sure, I know all about that, but this is different. You see, Lori, when Pa sold the farm, he got it in Federal money, not Confederate. So I've got all that, and now whoever marries me, why, he can take it and buy almost any farm he wants."

From outside came the yelping of a dog that had apparently treed something, and Charlie looked out the window. "That's that dog next door. He'd make a pretty good possum hound if I could just get him out in the woods. Look, he's done treed that yellow cat that lives across the street."

But Lori was more interested in Charlie's marital ideas. Clasping her hands tightly together, she said, "Charlie, I need to talk to you. You just don't understand that a man wouldn't be at all interested in what you're saying."

Charlie seemed genuinely surprised. "Why, certain he would! I've got the money to buy a good farm. I can work as good as any man. Drake would be glad to get a deal like that."

Lori felt helpless. "Charlie, a man wants more than a farm, and somebody to plow, and . . . there are other things."

"Like what?"

"Why, I mean like . . . well, like . . ." Lori suddenly bogged down, for she did not know where to start. Finally she said, "Well, like romance."

"I don't know much about that," Charlie said. "But I'll do everything that has to be done to be a good wife."

After the girl left to split more wood, Lori sat at the table for some time in a daze. *She's headed for a terrible fall. I hope she doesn't say anything to Drake about this. She's so straightforward and says whatever comes to her mind.* Then she spoke aloud. "I don't know how to help her, and I'm pretty sure Drake is not going to like it!"

Rosie came to a dead stop and grabbed Drake's arm, jerking him around and pointing at a shop window. "Look, that's just what I been lookin' everywhere for!"

Drake was in a hurry to get to Lori's house, but he stopped long enough to see that Rosie was staring at a display of bottles. He read the advertisement and then scowled in disgust. "Rosie, you don't need any more medicine! You got enough now to stock a store."

"But you know how my heart is. It ain't good at all," Rosie complained. "I been meanin' to get some of this for some time. Come on in, now." He hauled Drake into the shop, and when the clerk came up— a small man with a balding head—he said, "I want some of that Dr. Eckels Australian Auriclo."

The clerk grinned. "Yes, sir. How much do you want?"

"I better have three or four bottles."

The clerk quickly gathered the bottles together and held up one. "According to what this says, this'll do almost anything for you, sir."

Rosie took the bottle and read the label. "It's good for shortness of breath, fluttering, palpitation, irregularity or intermediate pulse, and an oppressed feeling in the chest. Well, I got all them symptoms," he said with vigor. "Ain't that right, Drake?"

Drake had long since given up trying to cure Rosie of his imaginary illnesses. "Just buy the stuff and let's go!" he said.

Rosie reached down into his pocket and pulled out a roll of Confederate bills. He paid for the patent medicine, and as the two soldiers went outside he said, "Now, I'm gonna get my heart fixed up at last."

Drake knew that there was nothing at all wrong with Rosie's heart. He had seen him go through battles that put most men past their endurance—without even breathing hard.

At the Holcomb house, Lori welcomed them, and Charlie came hurrying in from the yard where she had been feeding the chickens.

Rosie made a point of walking over and shaking hands with Charlie. "Hello there, Charlie," he said. "You're lookin' mighty fine."

"Hi, Rosie. I'm glad you came. You been doin' any fightin' with the Rebels?"

"Oh, no," he said. "They're all on the run. I did hear that there was gonna be some fightin' back in Tennessee where General Hood's gone, but all we got to do is set in Atlanta here and be sure the Rebels don't come back."

"I got some buttermilk, Rosie. Come on, and I'll get it for you."

"That sounds good. Buttermilk's good for an upset stomach."

Charlie looked at the tall soldier. "Is your stomach upset?"

"Well, it ain't *now*, but it might be. But if I drink that buttermilk, it won't be, will it now?"

He followed her into the kitchen, where Charlie poured him a tall glass of buttermilk and watched him drink it with relish. Then he pulled a medicine bottle out of his pocket and said, "Look at that. I got me some new heart medicine."

"I didn't know anything was wrong with your heart. You sure don't look like it. You're such a big, fine-lookin', strappin' fella."

Rosie stared at her with astonishment. He knew that in fact he was tall, gangly, and not at all handsome. "Been a long time since someone said that I was fine-lookin'. I guess not since my mama said it back when I was a baby sittin' in the cotton row." He drank the last of the buttermilk and grinned. "Maybe they got some medicine to make you good-lookin'."

"You look good enough to me. I sure like tall, lanky fellas. They look so much better than the little, short, stubby ones."

"Well, I'm tall enough, I reckon." He studied her, admiring the rosiness of her cheeks. She had very attractive features too. Her lips were red, and her eyes were large and widely spaced. He admired especially the unusual, curly brown hair. "What have you been doin' with yourself, Charlie?" he asked.

Soon they were deep in conversation at the kitchen table. Rosie, who was rather good at getting information out of people, found out many things about this young woman. Finally he said, "I might come callin' on you sometime."

"Callin' on me? Why, you're here now."

"No, I mean like a young man callin' on a young lady. I ain't ever done much of that, but I guess I could get into practice. Maybe you could put on a dress, and we could go to downtown and let 'em see what we look like."

Charlie smiled. "I don't know about the dress. I've only got one, and I haven't had it on for two years."

"You haven't had on a dress for two years?"

"No, been pretty busy with the farm. Oh, I mean except for church. Course, I wear it to church every time I go."

Rosie thought that most young women would not have been satisfied with one dress, but he was learning things about Charlie, and he liked what he saw.

Later on, Drake and Lori and Rosie and Charlie went into the sitting room and looked at old pictures in Mrs. Holcomb's family album. As usual, such pictures were amusing, and the four of them enjoyed them very much. Afterward, Lori said, "How about some music?"

"That would be mighty fine," Rosie said with enthusiasm. "Drake, play us a tune on that fiddle over there."

Drake picked up the violin from the table. He fingered it for a moment, tuned it, then began playing a lively song.

"Why, I know that," Charlie said. "We sing it all the time around Macon."

"Let's hear you sing it," Rosie said.

At once Charlie began singing a folk song that was popular all over the South. She had a clear, powerful, and very sweet voice.

When she finished, Lori said, "Charlie, you have a beautiful voice!"

"Well, I just sing mostly church songs."

"Then sing one of those," Lori said.

Without any accompaniment at all, Charlie began "Amazing Grace." She sang it simply and without the benefit of musical training, but the beauty of her voice filled the room.

When she was through this time, Rosie said, "That do beat all I ever heard! You're a regular canary!"

For the rest of the evening Drake played and sang, many times accompanied by Charlie. She did not know all the songs he did, but when their voices did join, they blended together very sweetly.

But as the evening went on, Drake grew restless. Charlie had not been more than three feet away from him for two hours. He finally whispered to Lori, "Can't we get away from these two? That Charlie, she's worse than a chigger!"

"Don't say that, Drake. She's very much alone."

"I can't help that. I didn't take her to raise."

The evening finally came to an end, and the two men reluctantly rose to leave. They said their good-byes to the girls and started down the street. They had not gone more than ten feet before they heard Charlie's voice.

"Drake—wait a minute!"

He turned with some surprise, and Charlie came bounding up and looked into his face. She seemed nervous, and her lips trembled a little, but she said firmly, "I got somethin' to tell you, Drake."

"What is it, Charlie?"

"Well, when Pa sold the farm in Macon," she said, "he got the sale price of it in Federal money. I got it all. We ain't spent hardly none of it, me and Pa. Well, now he's gone and buried, and I got to do somethin'."

Drake could not imagine what in the world Charlie was leading up to. He glanced at Rosie, who appeared equally puzzled. "What is it you want to do?"

"I want you and me to marry up, Drake—and then we can take the money, and we can buy us a farm."

Drake's jaw dropped. He was aware that Rosie had gasped. He looked carefully at Charlie to see if she was joking—and saw that she was not.

"It's almost five hundred dollars, Drake—in Union money. We can buy a place with a house on it, and a barn, and some stock. And I can plow as good as any man. Together, you and me could have a good farm."

Drake had faced many a crisis but nothing like this. He pulled his handkerchief out and wiped his brow, which suddenly seemed to be covered with sweat. He looked over to Rosie for support, but the tall, gangling soldier looked to be so stunned he could not speak.

At last Drake said firmly, "Charlie, that's not the way it's going to be. We don't even *know* each other. I appreciate your offer, but I'm just not thinking of getting married right now. Good night, Charlie."

He turned and walked away as quickly as he could.

Drake did not see the tears come into Charlie's

eyes, but Rosie did. Rosie reached out and took her hand. "Don't feel bad, Charlie. It just came as a shock to him."

"He don't want me."

"You're a fine girl, and you'll find somebody someday. I'm afraid Drake and you wouldn't get along too well anyhow. He's kind of a high flier."

"What's that mean?"

"It means he's had lots of girlfriends. He's real popular, bein' a musician and all, and besides, he's in love with Miss Lori."

"He is?"

Rosie saw that the girl was totally taken unaware by this.

"I thought he just liked her," Charlie said simply. "Guess he thinks I'm a regular fool." She turned away from him and went inside.

Rosie watched her go. Then he ran and caught up with Drake, who was still walking rapidly. "Wait a minute, Drake."

Drake turned to him. "Did you ever hear of such a thing, Rosie?"

"No, I never did."

"She must be crazy!"

"No, she's not crazy. She just hasn't had as many breaks as some other folks have."

"Well, she's just got to get *that* idea out of her head! Do you think she understood when I said no?"

"She's real cut up about it. I could see that."

"I wouldn't even *consider* marrying that girl."

"I don't know about that, but I do know one thing."

"What?"

"I know she offered you all she had and didn't ask for much in return."

Drake stared at him, then shook his head. "It's crazy, and I don't want to hear any more about it."

Knowing Drake's stubbornness, Rosie said no more. But as they walked on, he kept seeing the hurt look on Charlie Satterfield's face, and he thought, *Drake's gonna have to be careful, or he'll hurt that girl real bad.*

8

A Proposal

Charlie plunged on out in front of him. "Hurry up, Rosie! They can't be far ahead."

They had come to the woods with a borrowed set of guaranteed possum hounds, and now that the sun was falling in the sky, Rosie was hot, sweaty, and scratched from head to toe by briars. Panting, he struggled free from the clinging vines that reached out and grabbed at him. "Wait up for me, will you, Charlie? I can't get through this blasted brush!"

Charlie turned and laughed when she saw him scrambling awkwardly along the path. "I've got to give you some lessons in possum hunting, Rosie," she said. Placing her hands on her hips, she waited until he came up to her. She made a rather fetching picture standing there. When she pulled off her straw hat, her brown curls sprang up at once, caught in the late afternoon breeze.

"You sure are somethin' on a trail!" he exclaimed. He took a deep breath. "I thought I'd been on some hard trails before, but I never saw anybody that could follow a pair of coon dogs like you can."

His praise brought a flush to Charlie's smooth, round cheeks. She blinked at the compliment but then put it off by saying, "I guess anybody that's been out in the woods chasin' possums since they were four years old, like I been, ought to learn a little somethin'."

Suddenly the plaintive howl of a dog sounded from up ahead. "They've treed him! Come on, Rosie!" She ran through the woods like a young deer.

Rosie followed as best he could. He found her standing under a huge persimmon tree, staring up into the branches. The dogs were wild, barking and standing on their hind legs and trying to climb the tree.

"Will you fellas shut up!" Rosie said. He leaned against the tree and wiped his brow with a red bandanna from his back pocket. "A man in my condition hadn't ought to go around chasin' possums through the woods in this heat!"

Charlie turned to him. "Maybe you ought to take another one of those pills," she suggested, her full lips curving up in a smile.

Sensing he was being teased, Rosie stuffed his handkerchief back into his pocket. "You just don't understand a man who's got health problems like I have," he said. "Why, I remember just two years ago the doctor told me I didn't have two weeks to live."

"Did you die?"

"No, I didn't die, but I thought I was going to. I had to take nearly a quart of liver medicine. Worst tastin' stuff I ever had. Anything that tasted that bad *had* to be good, though. So it cured me all up." He peered into the upper branches of the tree. "I think I see him up there. One of us will have to climb up and knock him out."

"How are you at climbing trees?" Charlie asked.

"Not very good. It's not good for my rheumatism."

"You and your rheumatism! You're one of the strongest men I ever saw, Rosie. But I like to climb trees. Here, give me a boost up to that first branch."

Rosie shrugged but leaned over and picked her up bodily so that she could reach the lower limb.

Charlie gasped. "I didn't mean for you to *throw* me up here!" She grasped the branch, pulled herself up on it with an acrobatic motion, and grinned back down at him. "Watch out, now. When I knock him loose, you catch him before the dogs tear him up."

She started upward into the foliage, and Rosie stood on the ground trying to follow her progress. The tree was tall, however, and the girl disappeared into the upper regions of the branches.

"Do you see him?"

"It's not a him. It's a her, and she's got a whole passel of little babies on her back, hangin' onto her tail."

"Well, toss her down. The little ones will make good eatin' too."

"Ain't gonna do that! Not with a mama."

Charlie suddenly reappeared, stepping from branch to branch and easily climbing down.

When she reached the bottom limb, she said, "Here I come!" Without waiting, she launched herself into the air, and Rosie barely had time to throw his hands up. She struck him in the chest, knocking him backwards, and when he sprawled on the ground, she fell with him.

"*Wuffff!*" Her weight knocked the breath out of him. Looking up, he saw her dark eyes laughing at him, and at the same time he became aware that she was not at all like any of the young men he had gone possum hunting with.

Suddenly Charlie's cheeks flamed red. She scrambled up, stammering, "I—I didn't mean to do that, Rosie! Are you hurt?"

Slowly he sat up, braced himself, and rose to his feet. He was rather embarrassed about the whole thing himself. "I guess I'll live through a couple more clean shirts," he muttered finally. "You sure are a funny girl, Charlie. I never saw another one like you."

Charlie looked up at him. "What do you mean? Because I don't wear dresses?"

"Well, there's that—but you don't *act* like a girl. Most girls I know would never think about going possum hunting, and they wouldn't do what you just did—knock a fella down by jumping out of a tree at him."

He saw hurt come into her eyes.

"I'm sorry I can't be more what I ought to be. But I been raised so much like a boy, I guess I just think like one." Her curls swung in the breeze. "I wish I *was* a boy. They have a lot more fun than girls."

"I'm glad you're not!" Rosie declared. "Plenty of ugly, hairy-legged boys around. What we need is more nice-looking girls like you."

She looked up again, as though to see if he was teasing. "I know I'm not pretty like Lori is," she said, "and I haven't had much of a chance to learn how to put on pretty clothes. But I bet she can't plow like I can."

"I bet she can't either." Rosie grinned. Then he looked at the sky. "It's gettin' dark. We better get back. Not ladylike for a girl to stay out after dark with a soldier." He added, "You know how soldiers are. Always romancing girls."

Charlie was walking along with her long, free strides. She gave the lanky soldier a questioning glance. "Do you romance girls, Rosie?"

"Well, not as much as Drake. Fellas as homely as I am is not likely to be hangin' around girls much."

"Did you ever have a sweetheart?"

"I thought I had one once, but a better-lookin' fella came along and took her away from me."

Charlie thought about this. "I bet the one she got wasn't as nice as you."

The two walked through a stand of pines where the needles had fallen for years unharvested and untouched so that their steps made no sound at all.

As they continued, Rosie was amazed that Charlie seemed able to name every bird, every bush, every plant in the forest. "You sure do know the woods," he said. "I was raised mostly in a small town. Although my folks farmed for a long time."

"Did you like farming?"

"Sure did. I like it better than anything I've done since."

"So do I. I like everything about it. I like breaking up the land in the spring and puttin' the seed in. Then you wait, and pray for rain, and for lots of sun—and then one day little, tiny green tongues start coming up. There's nothin' like it, is there, Rosie?"

Rosie said, "I like it, but not everybody does. Pretty hard to work all year on a crop, and then have the bugs eat it up, or the floods take it, and just lose it all."

"That's just part of it," Charlie said firmly. "When that happens, you just wait until the next year and try again." They talked about farming a while longer, and then she changed the subject. "Tell me some more about Drake."

"Drake? Well, he's all kinds of a fella. Good

lookin', as you can see, and can play a fiddle. Can do just about anything."

Charlie digested that, then said, "I guess he's had lots of sweethearts."

"Quite a few."

The brief answer did not seem to satisfy her. "I bet none of his sweethearts had a farm like I'm going to have. That ought to be in my favor, don't you think, Rosie?"

Rosie did not answer at once. He walked along slowly, letting her match his stride. "It ought to, I guess—if he wants to farm."

"Didn't he ever farm? Didn't he grow up on one?"

"No, his folks ran a store. He's mostly a town fella, Drake is. He likes his comfort."

The news seemed to depress Charlie, but then she brightened. "He'll like it if we get a nice house."

Rosie said slowly, "Charlie, have you ever thought that there might be more to gettin' married than havin' a place to go to?" When she turned to look at him, he threw his hands apart in a helpless gesture. "I mean, after all, two people don't live together for all their lives just to have a farm, or a house in town, or a business. I mean, there's more to it than that."

"Oh, I know," Charlie said. "Miss Lori talked to me about that. About romance, you mean."

"Yes, about romance. A fella likes a little romance in his courtin'. Don't you?"

"I don't know. I never had any."

"Didn't any fellas come hang around you back in Macon?"

"Why, no. Well, maybe some of 'em did, but I knew they wasn't serious. They was after the town girls or the ones that had pretty dresses and knew how to dance. Mostly they let me alone."

"I think you better study about how to make yourself more like other girls. If you're gonna catch a fella like Drake—you gotta use the right bait."

"What do you mean—bait?"

"A fish don't bite a bare hook, does he? You got to put a nice, juicy worm on there."

"Are you callin' me a worm?"

Rosie laughed aloud. "Of course not! But a worm's what draws the fish, and you know what draws fellas like Drake. You just said it. Fancy dresses and learnin' how to be especially nice to a fella . . ."

"How would *you* want a girl to behave if you was lookin' for one?"

"Me? Well now, I'm different from Drake. I'd just as soon go possum huntin' with you as go to any old dance. But lots of fellas want a girl to tell 'em how handsome they are and smile a lot at 'em. Just stuff like that."

"Maybe I can try to do some of that," Charlie said. "It don't seem to come natural, though. You'll help me, won't you, Rosie?"

"I can't do none of that for you. I can just tell you what I think." He hesitated, then said, "But I sure wouldn't want you to make a mistake. You haven't had much experience, Charlie, and Drake's had a lot. That could be a bad combination."

"What do you mean?"

"I mean, some fellas would take advantage of a girl."

"I know that. I've seen enough of it, I guess. Although it's never been tried on me."

"Yeah, but you're just practically throwing yourself at Drake, saying, 'Here I am, take me.' If a fella didn't have any honor, he might take you up on that, then leave you flat."

Charlie's cheek flamed. "I would never do anything wrong, and I don't think Drake would either."

"I just want you to be sensible. You're a good Christian girl, and just remember that."

Suddenly Charlie reached over and took Rosie's hand. She squeezed it and then held it in both of hers. "You're a good friend, Rosie. I never had a friend like you. I appreciate you helping me out."

Rosie was very conscious of the girl's warm, strong hands and of her large, winsome eyes. He wanted to touch the curls that adorned her head but knew that would be a mistake. "Charlie," he said finally, "I just want you to have the best."

"I tell you, Rosie, you got to keep that girl away from me! She's driving me crazy!"

Drake had been walking guard duty when Rosie suddenly appeared out of the darkness. He'd been so startled he raised his musket and almost pulled the trigger.

"Give the password!"

It turned out Rosie didn't know the password, and Drake glared at him, saying, "You're gonna get yourself killed, jumpin' out of the dark like that! What's the idea, Rosie?"

"Got to talk to you, Drake."

"Can't it wait till tomorrow?"

"I don't think so. We better talk now. You just go on walkin'. I'll walk along beside you."

"All right. What is it, then?" Drake resumed his patrol. He hated guard duty as he hated most things about the army. Actually he was glad Rosie had shown up, because he was growing lonesome and the hours seemed to drag. "Where have you been?" he asked the rangy soldier.

"Been over to see Charlie."

"Did you see Lori?"

"Sure, I saw Miss Lori. She gave me a piece of apple pie."

"Did you bring any back for me?"

"Nope, I ate it all. That was the last piece too."

"Rosie! You're always fussin' about how sick you are, and then you eat like a starving wolf! How did she look?"

"Charlie?"

"Lori!"

"I didn't come over to talk about Lori. You and Royal talk enough about her. I came to talk about Charlie."

And that was when Drake said, "You got to keep that girl away from me! She's driving me crazy!"

"Drake, I want you to listen to me," Rosie said. "You're not acting right about Charlie."

Drake whirled to face him. "*I'm* not acting right? *She's* the one who's not acting right. She follows me everywhere I go. I can't turn around without her being underfoot. She doesn't have any pride at all, and she doesn't know a thing!"

"That's right," Rosie said quickly. "She *doesn't* know anything, Drake. She hasn't had a chance to. That pa of hers, he treated her like a boy and made her feel like a boy, and now she doesn't know how a girl ought to act. But that's not her fault."

"It's not my fault either!" Drake snapped.

When he started marching again, Rosie followed alongside. "Look, I know she's aggravatin', and I know you're not interested in her. But she can't understand that. If she'd been brought up like a girl,

91

she'd know these things. But all she knows is she likes you, and she thinks you ought to like her."

"Did she tell you about the farm she's going to buy me?" Drake asked.

"Sure she did, and you ought to be grateful for it."

"Rosie, you know I don't *like* farms. I don't like cows, or chickens, or plowing, or anything else about farms. If I ever get out of this army, I'm gonna go to a big city. Maybe San Francisco—or even New York —where something's happening."

"That's all right, Drake. You may do that, but you got to figure out some way to do it without breakin' Charlie's heart."

"I got all I can do to beat Royal out. I think he's gettin' the inside track with Lori. Look, if you want to do some good, just go to that girl and tell her that it's useless and to leave me alone."

"She wouldn't believe me, but she'd believe you."

"All right. I'll tell her then."

"Wait a minute." Rosie reached out and pulled him to a stop. "I don't like the way you said that. You got to be gentle with her. You could hurt her real bad."

Drake stared into the darkness at his friend. He liked Rosie, but his nerves were on edge. He hated the army. He wanted out! If it had not been for Lori, he might have deserted long ago. "Look, you'll just have to tell her yourself. I can't do it to suit you, and I've already tried to hint around every way I know that I'm not interested in any girl in overalls."

"She's a fine girl, Drake."

"That may be, but she's not for me. Now, I don't want to hear any more about it. Either you talk to her, or I'll tell her. And you could probably do it better than I could."

Rosie stood in the darkness as Drake marched off. Then he turned and slowly made his way back to his tent, pulled off his shoes, undressed, and stretched out on his cot. For a long time he lay there, thinking about girls who hunted possums. "I never saw another one like her," he whispered, "but she sure is headed for a fall."

As soon as Royal walked into the house, Lori knew that something had brought him there other than just a visit. "Why, hello, Royal. You're off duty tonight?"

"I got Ira Pickens to fill in for me. I had to talk to you, Lori."

"Come on into the kitchen. I was shelling some peas."

"No, let's go into the sitting room."

"Sitting room?" she said with surprise. "All right." She led the way into the front room and turned up the lamp. It lit the room with a flickering, yellow glow. "Sit down, Royal. Is something wrong?"

Royal bit his lip and remained standing. "Yes, something is wrong, Lori." He was not much taller than average, but Lori was so small that she had to look up. He studied her for a moment, then said, "You probably know what I'm going to say."

Instantly Lori did know what Royal was going to say. Her heart began to beat faster, and she twisted her hands together nervously. But she said, "I . . . I guess you'll just have to tell me."

Royal took her hands and held them in his. "You know me pretty well, Lori. I'm not flashy like Drake.

I'm not tall like he is, and I can't play any instruments. I'm just pretty average."

Lori sensed this was very hard for him. "I don't think you're average, Royal," she said quietly.

"You don't?"

"Of course I don't. I've always thought you were one of the finest boys I ever met."

"Then that makes what I want to say easier." Royal hesitated only for a moment. "I love you, Lori," he said quietly. "I want to marry you someday and spend the rest of my life with you. I want us to grow old together and have grandchildren around our knees. All I can say is, I'll love you as long as I live, and you'll never know meanness from me. Lori, will you marry me?"

For a long time Lori had been expecting this, not knowing what she would say. She was drawn to Drake's good looks and quick wit. But as Royal Carter stood before her, she knew she wanted more than good looks and quick wit for the rest of her life.

She took a deep breath and voiced her decision. "Yes," she whispered, "I'll marry you, Royal. I've loved you for a long time, I think. But now I know you're the only man I would ever even think of marrying."

Royal's face lit up. He drew her forward, and his lips came down on hers. "I didn't think you'd say yes. I was afraid you were in love with Drake."

"Sometimes a girl has a hard time herself, knowing she has to choose. Drake may make some girl a fine husband, but it won't be me."

When Royal left, Lori walked upstairs to see if Mrs. Holcomb was all right. She found the old lady barely awake but in some pain. This happened often lately. She quickly picked up a bottle of brown fluid and a spoon.

"Can you sit up, Aunt Grace, and take this?" She gave the patient the medicine and helped her to lie down again. "Now you'll sleep. But before you do, I have something to tell you."

Grace's lips barely moved as she said, "I'll bet I know what it is. You're going to marry that soldier —the short one."

"That's right," Lori said. "How did you know it wasn't the tall one?"

The medicine had begun to take effect, but Mrs. Holcomb whispered, "You had something in your eyes for Royal that you never had with Drake . . ."

Lori thought then that her aunt had gone to sleep, but Mrs. Holcomb spoke again. "Tell Charlie to be careful about Drake."

"I will," Lori said, "but I don't know if she'll listen."

9

"What's Going On?"

Cecil Taylor was pleased that Leah was paying him so much attention. He had been attracted to her ever since she first came to Richmond and now was even more so. As the two walked together along the street, he glanced at her, thinking how pretty she looked, and tried to find some way to say so. Actually, Cecil Taylor was very shy.

He was thin in his first lieutenant's uniform. (It was new enough that he was still proud of it.) He glanced at their reflection in a shop window and thought they made a very handsome couple.

"Let's go see if they have some ice cream, Leah."

"Ice cream?" Leah turned to look where Cecil was pointing.

A sign advertised that delicacy.

"Let's," she said. "I haven't had any ice cream in a long time."

Leah's plan to make Jeff jealous seemed to be working exactly as she had hoped. Almost every day for the past two weeks, Cecil had found some excuse to come to the house and visit her.

From time to time, Jeff would come by and see Cecil sitting on the front porch—or find her gone walking with him while Eileen kept Esther. She had noticed that the sweeter she was about it, the more Jeff seemed to be irritated.

Leah and Cecil went into the shop and were soon seated at a table with two large bowls of vanilla ice cream in front of them.

The proprietor, a small, heavy woman with a pair of bright, black eyes, smiled at them. "You better enjoy that ice cream," she said. "We've used up about the last of the ice that we have in the ice house." Her gaze grew troubled, and she turned away, saying, "It seems like it's almost the last of something every time I turn around."

"This is good ice cream," Cecil said to Leah, "but I bet you could make better."

Leah put a spoonful of the smooth dessert into her mouth, swallowed it, and then smiled sweetly. "And I bet you could make better ice cream too, Cecil."

He laughed. "I never made ice cream. We always had the slaves do that. I tried to turn the freezer once, and my arm just absolutely gave out. Someday—" he grinned at her "—someday they'll learn to hook up an ice cream freezer to a steam engine or maybe a water wheel."

"Oh, they'll never do that," Leah said. Then she said, "You look so handsome in your uniform, Cecil."

A blush spread over his countenance. "I don't know about that," he said. "But I do know you look very pretty in that dress."

Leah was wearing a powder blue dress with dark blue ribbon woven into the neckline and along the hem. She and Eileen had worked hard on it for several days, and the result was just right. "Oh, do you like this dress?" she said coyly.

"I like you in almost anything," Cecil said. He swallowed hard. Then he said, "We've gotten to be real good friends in the last couple weeks, haven't we?"

Leaning toward him, Leah said, "Yes, we have. It's been wonderful having you come to see me, and we have had good times."

She was pleased to see how easy it was to keep Cecil happy. *If only Jeff were as easygoing as Cecil,* she thought, when they had finished their ice cream and were leaving the shop. *Life would be a whole lot easier. But in just a few more days, I'll have Jeff exactly where I want him.*

"I don't know what you think you're doing, Leah," Jeff said, tension in his voice. He stood over her as she sat in Uncle Silas's front porch swing. He drew his lips into a thin line.

"I don't know what you mean, Jeff." Leah looked up innocently.

She had come home with Cecil to find Jeff inside talking to his father. Cecil had not stayed long, and when he left, Leah sat down on the porch. Jeff had come out almost at once.

Smoothing her dress, she said, "Why don't you sit down, Jeff? You look all bothered."

"I *am* bothered," Jeff said, but he did not sit down.

Sticking his hands in his pockets, he teetered back and forth. He seemed to be trying to hold onto his temper. "What's going on with all this attention you're paying to Cecil?"

"I wasn't aware that I was paying any attention to him."

Jeff stared at her. "You've taken up lying too, have you?"

Leah's temper flared. "I wasn't lying!"

"You were too! I've seen that look in your eyes since you were four years old! Every time you tell a fib, it's like a sign saying, 'Look at me, I'm lying.' You know good and well you've been flirting with Cecil!"

"That's a fine way to talk to me!"

"Somebody needs to talk to you!" Jeff said with exasperation. "You're acting like the world's worst flirt, and you know it!"

Leah felt a pang of guilt, for Jeff had put his finger on something that had been troubling her. Several times she had looked at Cecil and thought that she really was mistreating him. But then she'd justified her actions by telling herself that he liked her as a friend, and she liked him, and there was nothing wrong with having a good time together.

Still, Jeff's words stung, and she said defensively, "I don't see why you care. You're always going to see Lucy!"

"Are we going to argue about that again? Are you still angry with me because she kissed me after that play?"

"I don't care if she kisses you. That's your business and hers."

Jeff put out his hands in a gesture of despair. "What's happened to you, Leah? You didn't use to be like this. If this is growing up, then it doesn't become you very much."

"I *am* growing up! Maybe you haven't noticed," Leah snapped. "Boys are all alike. They think they can pay attention to any girl that comes along—but you just let a girl *look* at a boy, and she's a flirt!"

"I don't know why I waste my time with you," he said. "You're growing up all right, but I'm not sure I like all the changes I see."

Leah decided that this had gone on long enough. She stood and put a hand on his arm. "Jeff, don't be angry with me," she whispered.

He seemed so tall and strong, and despite the fact that he wore only the uniform of a plain soldier, he still looked very good. His coal-black hair glistened, and she thought, *Jeff just doesn't know how good-looking he is. And I guess that's a good thing.* Aloud she said, "Cecil is a nice boy. He gets lonesome, I suppose. You're just jealous."

Jeff glared, anger growing in his face, and Leah was quick to see that of all the things she might have said, this was the last to make the quarrel disappear.

"*Jealous?* That's something for you to say! You practically turn green every time you see me with Lucy, and now you're saying *I'm* jealous? I give up! But I'm telling you this, Leah. You're making a mistake flirting with Cecil like that."

"You really know everything, don't you?" she taunted.

"I know Cecil's a nice fellow, and I know you don't really care anything about him, but *he* doesn't know that. Some day your chickens are going to come home to roost."

Wheeling, Jeff leaped off the porch to the ground and practically ran toward the road.

Leah watched him go and felt miserable.

Then she went inside and wandered through the house until she came upon Eileen sitting in the parlor, sewing. Sitting down, she said, "Eileen, did you have trouble when *you* were growing up?"

Smiling, Eileen put down her sewing and came over to sit beside her. Putting an arm around Leah, she said, "A girl needs a mother, Leah. Fortunately,

100

I had a good one, but you're separated from yours now, and that's a shame."

"Jeff and I just had a fight."

"Oh? What about?"

Leah suddenly discovered she wanted to tell Eileen what was happening—but at the same time, she didn't. "Oh," she said, "he's jealous of Cecil."

"Should he be?"

"I—I don't know what you mean."

"You and Jeff have been friends for a long time, haven't you?"

"Oh, yes. All our lives."

"And you like him probably as well as any boy you ever knew, I would think. I've seen that in you."

"That's true. Jeff and I have always been close."

"And yet you've been going around with Cecil every chance you get. I wonder why that is?"

Leah felt her cheeks burn, and she put her hands over them. "Oh, Eileen, I don't know. I thought I might make Jeff a little bit jealous."

"That's very dangerous. I think you might be sorry about that."

Her words were very close to what Jeff had said, and Leah felt tremendously uncomfortable.

10

Rosie Steps In

The camp for the Federal troops was south of Atlanta. Tents had been set up, and since the force was small, the duties were heavy. Most of the men had to stand guard at various times. Nevertheless, since there had been no uprising among the citizens and no likelihood that Johnston's army would return to give them trouble, discipline relaxed as the days passed.

Drake had not forgotten his humiliation on the wooden horse, and he had been prohibited from leaving camp by the lieutenant. Day after day, he saw Royal go and come, and this made him sullen.

One afternoon, at the end of the first week of September, he looked up from where he was sitting on a camp stool in front of his tent, and what he saw sent a shock through him.

"Oh, no! It's that blasted Charlie!" He got up and would have escaped, but she called out, "Hello, Drake!" and reluctantly he returned to his place.

Charlie was still wearing her overalls, albeit she was sporting a pair of new low-heeled boots that looked much better than the heavy shoes she had first worn. She came marching across the parade ground, catching the eye of most of the soldiers who were off duty.

Drake took a desperate look around and saw them grinning and nudging one another with their elbows. Somehow the story had gotten out about how this girl wanted to buy herself a husband. Drake had accused Royal of spreading the tale, but Royal steadfastly denied it. Actually it turned out that Charlie herself let it slip to Walter Beddows, who could never keep a good story. Now Walter and the others began ambling toward where Charlie stood in front of Drake.

"I came to see you, Drake," she said brightly. She was wearing a new straw hat with a ribbon on top. She wore a new shirt under her overalls too. A bright red one.

Drake nodded shortly. "Hello, Charlie." He sought desperately for some way to escape but could think of nothing.

Charlie started talking about a fishing trip that she had just made. "I caught seven bullhead cats," she said, "and I'm going to cook 'em up for supper. I came to invite you, Drake."

"I can't leave camp," he said

"Oh, why not?"

"Because he's been a bad boy."

The voice came from behind Charlie, and she turned to see Walter Beddows, who was grinning broadly. Walter loved fun. He came closer and winked at the others. "None of the rest of us galoots have been lucky enough to capture a prisoner like you, Miss Charlie," he said. "Tell me now. Are there any more that I might go out and capture?"

Charlie looked at Drake uncertainly, clearly not understanding the joke. "I don't guess so," she said finally. "I was lucky he didn't shoot me. His gun didn't go off."

A laugh went around, and Walter said, "You mean you actually tried to pull down on this pretty girl? Why, Drake Bedford, I'm plumb ashamed of you!"

"Shut up, Walter!" Drake said. He suddenly saw Royal approaching and was sure the sergeant was on his way to Lori's house. He exploded. "Get out of here, girl! Go back home!"

A hurt look came into Charlie's eyes, and she lowered her head. "I just came to invite you—"

"You're always pestering me! I don't want you hangin' around me anymore! No man likes a woman chasin' after him. Now, get out of here and leave me alone!"

An angry murmur went around the small group of soldiers, but Drake didn't care. Well, he did care —he hated to hurt the girl's feelings—but he had had all he could take. Then he saw that she was watching him with tears in her eyes, and he opened his mouth to apologize.

But at that moment Rosie came up and put his hand on Charlie's shoulder. "Come along, Charlie," he said.

"No, I can go by myself." Two tears ran down her cheeks. She wiped them away with her sleeve, then said, "I'm sorry, Drake. I didn't mean to bother you." She walked away, a woeful figure, and silence fell over the circle of soldiers.

When she was out of hearing, Royal said, "I hope you're proud of yourself, Drake."

Drake doubled up his fists. "Shut up, or I'll bust you!" He knew if he hit a sergeant he would be riding the wooden horse again, but he was so upset that he didn't care.

"You can't hit a sergeant," Rosie said. He put himself between Drake and Royal and said over his shoulder, "Sergeant, would you mind leaving for a minute? I have something to say to Private Bedford."

Royal must have known instantly what was going to happen. It would be better for Drake to hit a private than a sergeant. Royal said, "All right," and walked off.

As soon as he was gone, Drake made his own move to leave. But he felt his arm grasped in a steely grip. He was whirled around to face Rosie, whose ordinary lazy manner was gone.

"Now, don't *you* start on me, Rosie!" Drake said, jerking his arm back.

"I'm not gonna start on you, Drake," Rosie said. "I'm gonna finish up on you!"

"What does that mean?"

"It means I'm gonna bust your nose, and black your eyes, and pound your gizzard," Rosie said calmly.

Drake blinked. Rosie was his best friend, and he could not believe what he was hearing. "You'd fight with me over that no-account girl?"

"That no-account girl," Rosie said, and he paused to unbutton his sleeve and push it up over his elbow, "is worth about a hundred of you." He carefully rolled up the other sleeve. "You want to take your whippin' here, or you want to step into the woods?"

Drake Bedford was a renowned fighter. He was strong and tall and quick. He had seen Rosie fight and knew that his friend was strong too, but there was no question in Drake's mind about how a conflict would come out. Still, he hated to fight Rosie, his only friend. "Butt out of this, Rosie. It's none of your business."

"I reckon when a no-account like you insults a lady in public, I'll just have to make it my business.

Now, get your hands up, Drake, because I am going to commence to stomp the daylights out of you!"

Drake laughed. "You couldn't whip your grandma!" He put his hands up and advanced. "I'm not gonna hurt you, Rosie, but I've got to show you that you can't run over me."

He threw a left that caught Rosie on the forehead and hurt his fingers.

Rosie simply reached out, grabbed that arm, and —before Drake could pull back—looped over a tremendous right that hit Drake in the mouth.

It was a disaster! Red stars, and yellow and green also, flashed before Drake's eyes. He tried to get away, but Rosie held firmly to his wrist. Another blow caught him, this time over his left eye. Pain ran through his head, and he felt blood flowing from his eyebrow. Rosie released his arm, and he staggered backward.

Wiping the blood from his face, he shouted, "I'll kill you, Rosie!"

"Then just fly right at it!" Rosie growled. His face was set.

Drake managed to slip under his next punch and catch Rosie with a hard right to the neck. It slowed Rosie down not one bit. The lean soldier waded forward, and suddenly, for Drake, the air was full of fist. He gave as many blows as he got, he thought, but there was something invincible about Rosie. Blows struck him in the face, on the chest, in the stomach, and then he realized that he was lying flat on his back.

"Get up, Drake."

Rosie stood over him, looking down at his skinned knuckles. "Any time you're ready to go apologize to Charlie, I'm willin' to stop."

Drake struggled to his feet. His face ached, and his ribs, yet he knew that he would never give up. He threw himself at Rosie again. The soldiers had made a ring about them, and repeatedly Rosie knocked Drake back into one of them, who would then shove him forward.

For Drake, time seemed to stand still. Finally he was on the ground and discovered that he could not get up. "My—legs won't work," he panted. "My blasted legs won't work. Wait a minute, and I'll fight you, Rosie . . ."

Rosie looked down at him. "You and me been friends for a long time, but I don't need a friend like you, Drake. Any man that would treat a woman like you treated Charlie, no amount of beatin's gonna help. Because your meanness," he said evenly, "ain't on the outside. It's on the inside! I always knew somethin' was wrong with you, and now I know that's it. Don't ever come at me to speak again, because I'm through with you!"

As Rosie turned around and walked off, rather unsteadily, Drake struggled to a sitting position, then to his feet. His eyes were swelling. One was closed completely. His uniform was torn, his fists were scraped, he could taste blood, and he hurt all over.

But what hurt worst of all was seeing Rosie disappear. Drake looked around and saw no friendship on the faces of his fellow soldiers. They all turned then and walked away from him, leaving him standing alone.

Drake staggered to the pump and washed his face. He looked down at his ripped, dirty uniform and then reeled away from the parade ground. He took the road that led to the woods just outside

Atlanta. Every step jolted his bruised body, and all he could think was, *I got to get away. I can't stand this anymore!*

11

A New Man

Royal met Rosie heading toward his tent, and one look at his bloodied face told the story. "Did you have it out with Drake?"

"Yes, I did, but I don't feel good about it." Rosie stood looking at the ground. "He's been my best friend for a long time, Royal."

"I know. It's hard to fight with a friend."

"I reckon it is."

"Where is he now?"

"Headed out somewhere. You better go catch him, Royal. He might desert, and the general would have him shot sure."

"I think you're right. Why don't you clean yourself up? I'm sorry this had to happen."

Royal broke into a run. Ahead he saw Drake, walking blindly along the line of tents and apparently headed for the woods.

"Drake!" he called out. "Wait a minute!" He caught up with the private and put himself directly in front of him. "Where are you going?"

"What difference does it make?"

"It makes a lot of difference if you get posted as a deserter!" Royal said. "You know what the general would do to you then."

"He'd have to catch me first!"

"That wouldn't be too hard to do. Look, we all make mistakes from time to time. We all have to learn how to say we're sorry."

"Is that what you want me to do? Come crawlin' back and say I'm sorry?"

"Not to me. To Charlie."

Drake hesitated, as though considering doing exactly what Royal was suggesting. But then he shook his head stubbornly. "I'll write her a letter sometime."

"Drake, I'm going tell you something else." Royal waited until Drake's eyes were fixed on him. "I've asked Lori to marry me, and she said that she would. I wanted you to hear it from me, not from somebody else."

At first Royal thought Drake would throw himself at him, and he stiffened, waiting for the charge.

But the fire in Drake's eyes died, and he took a deep breath. "Well, that makes you happy, doesn't it? You beat me out."

"No, beating you doesn't make me happy. I know what it's like to lose something you love. One of us had to get hurt, but I'm not happy about it."

After a moment Drake said, "All right, you've won. You don't have to stand around crowin' about it." He started off again toward the woods.

"Drake, wait a minute—"

"Leave me alone, Royal! Just leave me alone!"

Royal stood uncertainly, watching him go. He could not lay hold on the soldier and bring him back forcefully, and yet he was afraid that Drake would indeed desert. Slowly he turned back to camp, thinking, *If he doesn't come back soon, I'll send the squad out looking for him.*

Then Royal thought about the look on Drake's face when he had told him about his engagement to Lori. Aloud he said, "I guess I'd be just as bad if I'd been the one who lost her."

"We can't find him anywhere, sarge."

Royal looked up from where he was working on papers for the lieutenant to see Jay and Walter. It was morning. Drake had not returned, and Royal had sent the entire squad into the woods looking for him.

Walter said, "He didn't leave no sign that I could see. I don't know where he's gotten to." He bit his lip then. "I guess we were pretty hard on him."

"He treated that girl pretty bad," Jay said. "But I wouldn't want to see him desert. Not but one end to that."

Walter looked cautiously towards town. "Maybe he cut back and went into town somewhere. Maybe he's gone over to see Lori again."

The thought came to Royal that perhaps Jay was right. "That may be," he said. "I'll go check there, and the rest of you keep on looking. We've got to find him!"

At the time the squad was out searching desperately for him, Drake Bedford was lying flat on his back under a tree. He had wandered through the woods last night, finally coming across a small tavern where he bought several drinks of whiskey. The alcohol, raw and rank, had hit him hard, for he had eaten nothing. Then he'd gone back into the woods in another direction from camp, not knowing where he was. He went to sleep and had awakened this morning with the sun beating down on his face.

His head ached, his face was stiff and sore, and he knew that both eyes were a beautiful shade of purple. He lay still for a long time, and when he did move, his head felt as if a spike had been driven through it. Grunting with pain, he sat up and rested his back against the tree.

Overhead a pair of birds sang merrily, and Drake looked up and scowled. "Why do you have to be so blasted happy when I'm so miserable?" He had no strength to stand up and had never felt worse in his life. Carefully he wiggled his teeth, for he was certain that Rosie's mighty blows had knocked some of them loose. All seemed to be intact, however, and he dropped his hands to the ground and closed his eyes. Shame ran through him as he realized how he had behaved.

He began to review what had happened. "It seems like nothin' right has happened ever since I got in the army," he muttered. "Now I've lost Lori, made all the fellas in the squad hate me, my best friend has beat me up . . ." He tried to think of happier times.

And a strange thing took place. Drake had gone with Rosie once or twice to the revival meetings held for the soldiers. Now, out of nowhere, the words of one of the chaplains came to him almost as clearly as if spoken aloud. *"It is appointed unto man once to die, but after this the judgment."*

The sentence kept coming back to him again and again. And then he began to grow afraid. This was unusual, for Drake was a courageous man, even in battle. But now, somehow, a greater fear than he had ever known came over him. It was the fear of death.

Looking around, he felt foolish. The grass was green under him, the sky was blue, the trees stretched their branches upward, the birds were singing. There was no danger here. And yet Drake suddenly thought, *What if I should die in the next battle and had to face*

God? He knew the answer to that. He had heard enough preaching to know what happened to those who went out to meet God unprepared.

He saw that his hands were trembling. "I didn't know anything could make me do that," he said aloud. "What's wrong with me?"

Another Scripture came to mind. Again, he could almost hear the chaplain say it. *"Except ye repent, ye will all likewise perish."* And then immediately another: *"Except a man be born again, he cannot see the kingdom of God."*

Drake had never been one for introspection. He had never thought much about eternity, or God, or judgment, but he thought about them now. And the longer he sat under the tree, the worse it got. In desperation, he struggled to his feet and began to walk, hoping the mood would pass.

It did not pass, though. As he moved on, he found that his fear grew. Finally he looked up and said, "God, what's happening?"

The heavens were still blue and peaceful, but there was no peace in Drake. At last he lay down in the shade of a towering oak. It was quiet in the glade —no one else was there—yet somehow Drake knew that Someone *was* there. Looking to the sky again, he said, "God, what is it? What's happening to me?" Then he began to weep, something he had not done since he was a small boy.

"Drake, you're back!"

Royal leaped up from his cot and ran to grasp Drake's arm. "Thank God you've come back. I was afraid you were going to be posted as a deserter. Where in the world have you been?"

Drake was pale, and there was an odd look about him. "Hello, Royal," he said in a voice that was almost a whisper.

Royal said quickly, "Here, sit down. You look white as a sheet." He pushed Drake onto the cot, glad that Ira Pickens, his tent mate, was not there. "Are you all right?"

"Yes, I'm all right."

"I thought maybe you got hurt worse than we knew in the fight—and went out and fell down unconscious somewhere," Royal said. "The whole squad's been lookin' all over creation for you. We've covered for you, though. Nobody else knows you've been gone."

"Thanks, Royal. It was good of you—and all the other fellas too."

Royal sat down across from him. "So where have you been?" He studied the soldier's beaten features and noted that the eyes were clear although the bruises were violently colorful. "We've all been worried about you. We can't let the Devil have one of our own."

It was a saying that the soldiers often used.

Drake clasped his hands, then put them against his lips. He seemed to be thinking deeply. Then he said, "I guess the Devil almost got me. But he didn't."

"What does that mean?" Royal asked in bewilderment.

"It means I got out there all by myself in the woods, and something happened to me, Royal." Drake's voice was subdued. He tried to smile. "Ow, it hurts to smile! My lips are all cut."

"What have you got to smile about?"

"You'd think not much. I lost my girl, lost my best friend, got beat to pieces—but something happened to me out in those woods, Royal, and I know you'll be glad to hear it even though we haven't been friends."

Suddenly Royal thought he knew exactly what he was talking about. "Drake," he breathed. Leaning forward, he grabbed Drake's arms. "What happened out there?"

"I don't know exactly what to call it. I never felt so guilty in my whole life," he said. "And I couldn't run away from it either. And the longer it went on, the worse it got . . ."

"What happened then?"

"Well, I've heard enough sermons to know that Jesus is the only way to get saved. So I didn't know any better than just to call on Him—and I did, Royal. I was so miserable I was ready to blow my brains out. But then I called on God to forgive me for Jesus' sake, and I asked Him to do something with me. Well—" he tried another smile "—He said He would, and I believe He did."

"I'm glad. Real glad."

"Yeah, I knew you would be. You always tried to get me to find God, and I wouldn't do it. I was runnin' as hard as I could, but He caught up with me out in those woods."

"It's the best thing that could've happened to you, Drake. I think you were just one of those fellas that have to hit bottom before they call on God."

Drake was sober-faced. "I reckon that's right, Royal—and I sure hit bottom this time—but when I called on God, He was right there!"

12

Disaster for Leah

Jeff's sergeant sent him back from the lines at Petersburg to try to round up some food. The Southern troops were scraping the bottom of the barrel. Glad to be out of the monotony of the trenches, he hitched a scrawny, elderly horse to a light wagon and drove through the countryside. He managed to buy some vegetables and even a whole smoked ham, along with other various items.

As an afterthought, as he headed back down the road toward camp, Jeff stopped at a tall, white house marked by columns in front. This was Cecil Taylor's home. He knew Cecil's parents were highly sympathetic to the Confederacy. He drove around to the back, mounted the steps, and knocked.

It was not a slave but Cecil himself who opened the door. "Hey, Jeff. What are you doing here?"

Jeff blinked with surprise. "Why, hello, lieutenant," he said, remembering Cecil's officer status. "My sergeant sent me around the countryside to see if I could scare up some food. I thought maybe you might have a ham or something stored in the smokehouse that the fellas could have."

Cecil frowned. "Willikers, Jeff, I think we're running pretty low. But come along back. Surely we can find something."

"Don't mean to put you out, lieutenant."

"Oh, for crying out loud, Jeff—I'm *Cecil.* I feel like a phony anyhow, wearing this uniform." He strolled rapidly toward the smokehouse, and as Jeff followed he continued. "You've been in almost every battle since Bull Run, and I've never even heard a shot fired. I'm just a joke is all I am."

"Don't say that, Cecil," Jeff said quickly. "We all do what we're told to do. Evidently your officers think you're worth more here in Richmond, and someone has to do this part of the job."

Cecil shook his head but said no more until they got to the smokehouse. There he quickly pulled down several slabs of smoked meat. "Here. Take these back to your squad."

"I'll pay you for that, Cecil. All I've got is Confederate money, though."

"Oh, never mind. That stuff's not worth the paper it's printed on. Matter of fact, I heard they were even running out of paper to print the money on. Next thing, they'll be printing it on cornshucks."

Back at the wagon, Jeff pulled up the canvas and stored the meat safely. Turning back to Cecil, he smiled. "Sure do appreciate this a lot. And the fellas, they'll just be plumb glad to see it."

The lieutenant shrugged his shoulders slightly. "Don't mention it, Jeff." He paused, then said, "I been wanting to talk to you—about Leah."

Instantly Jeff tensed. He had always liked Cecil, had gotten along with him. He still liked him. He looked down at the young lieutenant, who was his age but two inches shorter than he was and very light in frame. He said, "Well, all right, go ahead, Cecil."

Cecil seemed terribly ill at ease. He scratched his head and stared off into the sky where a flight of blackbirds was making its noisy way toward a cornfield. Then he faced Jeff and nervously ran his hand through his chestnut hair. Finally he blurted out, "You know I've always liked Leah, but I thought the two of you were—you were real good friends always."

"That's right. We grew up together."

"That's what I mean. But of course, things are a little bit different now. We're all grown up. It's not like it was when you were kids."

"Yep. She reminds me of that all the time. Talks about how hard it is to grow up, and I think she's right. Not just for girls, but for boys too."

Cecil grinned and seemed much relieved. "I'm glad to hear you say that. But really, what I wanted to ask you—Jeff, do you mind my calling on Leah?"

Instantly Jeff understood what Cecil was saying. He also knew that Leah had no deep feelings for this boy, but it was not his place to say so. He shifted his feet in the dust and chewed his lip. "Well . . . like you say, Cecil, Leah and I are real good friends . . ."

"That's not what I mean. I mean, do you mind my *calling* on her? I'm pretty serious about her, you know."

"I see you are, Cecil—" Jeff sought desperately to find an answer for the lieutenant but could think of nothing wise to say. "As far as I'm concerned, you can call on her."

Relief washed across Cecil Taylor's face. He took Jeff's hand and pumped it. "I'm sure glad to hear you say that! I wouldn't want to cut in between you and Leah, but if that's the way you feel about it. Well—I feel a whole lot better!"

Jeff felt slightly foolish. He knew that Cecil cared much more for Leah than she knew—and he knew Leah cared much less for Cecil than *he* knew. Finally he said, "I've got to get back to Petersburg. I wish you good luck."

"Thanks, Jeff. That's like you. I really do think a lot of Leah."

"I thought you liked Lucy," Jeff said suddenly. "You two always seemed to be real close."

"Aw, you know how Lucy is. She's so pretty, and every young officer in the county is humming around her. She'd never pay any serious attention to me. Besides, we grew up together, and you know how that is. A boy and a girl grow up together, and they hardly ever get serious, do they?"

"Well . . . hardly ever," Jeff agreed. He climbed into the wagon, waved to Cecil, and said, "I'll give that bacon to the boys with all your love."

"All right, Jeff, and thanks."

As Jeff drove on, muttering, he pulled his hat down over his face to shade it from the blistering sun. "I don't know what he's thanking me for. It's almost like I was Leah's pa and he was askin' for permission to call on her." He slapped the reins on the skinny back of the horse. "Get up, horse. No sense loafin' around here."

Eileen was sitting in the grape arbor with Colonel Majors. He had hobbled out to enjoy the fresh air. September was still hot, and the shade from the vines provided welcome relief.

"By harry," he said, "it's good to be out again!"

She smiled and said quietly, "You need sunshine and exercise. You're very pale."

"Just let me get out a few more days, and I'll be ready to go back to the regiment."

A cloud passed across Eileen's face. She did not like to be reminded that soon Nelson would go back

119

and take his place in the trenches where men were dying every day. She knew it was a miserable, unromantic war fought in the mud, where death came when a man raised his head one inch too high. She also knew that Nelson Majors was the kind of man who would not shirk his duty—and was therefore the sort that usually managed to get himself wounded or killed.

Looking over at her, he said, "Don't worry about me. I'll last this war out. I've got to," he said. "I've got to change your name."

It had become a joke between them, this changing of her name as a symbol of their marriage. He took her hand and studied her face. "You have such beautiful hair. I always did like red hair."

"Red hair means a hot temper, so people say."

He laughed abruptly. "I've seen a little bit of that, and I expect to see more. That's all right. I like a woman with spirit."

They sat enjoying the breeze and watching the birds as they flew in the distance. Far off, a dog seemed to have treed something and was howling in long, mournful tones.

"If I was a little stronger, I'd go see what that dog has up a tree," he said.

"Better leave that to somebody else. You have better things to do, such as sitting here with me."

Nelson smiled. "You're pretty proud now that you've caught a prospective husband."

"Yes, I need somebody to boss around. Now I've got you and Esther—and even Jeff and Tom for a while."

Nelson leaned back, thoughtful. "I'm kind of worried about Jeff. It looks like he's off his feed."

120

"I think he and Leah are having some difficulties."

"Have you talked to Leah about it?"

For a moment Eileen considered sharing Leah's comments about her plan to make Jeff jealous. But then she knew she could not do that. It would violate a confidence. She put him off by saying, "You sit right where you are, and I'll make some tea."

Leah was helping in the kitchen when Eileen suddenly said, "Leah, I've been thinking about what you told me about Cecil, and I think you must be careful. It's very easy to hurt people."

Leah looked up, surprised. She trusted Eileen's opinion a great deal and admired her. But she said, "Oh, it's all right. Cecil doesn't really care about me."

"Are you sure about that?"

"He just likes to have a good time. We're just good friends."

Later in the day, Leah was in the garden picking bugs off the plants and sprinkling snuff on some of them, having heard that was good anti-insect protection. The snuff made her sneeze from time to time, and she wrinkled her nose. "I don't see how people can put this in their mouth!"

At that moment she heard a horse approaching. "Hello, Cecil," she called. "I'm out here in the garden!"

He tied the mare to the hitching post and joined her.

"You can help me pull bugs," she said.

Cecil grinned. "You're asking a soldier of the Confederacy to pick bugs off vegetables?"

"In that case, you can watch *me* pull bugs."

But she noticed that Cecil seemed nervous. She continued to the end of the row, then said, "That's enough bug pulling for one day. Come on, let's go down to the brook. I'll take off my shoes, and you can take off those hot boots, and we can go wading."

Leah led him to the narrow creek that circled the house like a crook, and soon she sat paddling her feet beneath the large hickory tree that shadowed the noisy stream.

Cecil didn't take his boots off. "I've got a hole in my sock," he said. "I wouldn't want you to see it."

She laughed, and they talked a while about little things.

Suddenly Cecil reached out and took her hand.

Leah was so surprised she didn't know what to say. She saw that he was struggling desperately to say something. "Is something wrong? It's not somebody killed in the war, is it, Cecil?"

"No—no, it's nothing like that. It's not bad news, Leah." He held onto her hand, then cleared his throat. "Leah, I want to tell you something."

"What—what is it, Cecil?"

"I want to tell you—" he cleared his throat again "—I want to tell you how much I admire you."

Leah gave him a startled look and said quickly, "How nice of you to say so, Cecil."

"No, it's more than that," he added, and his grip tightened on her hand. "It's more than admiration. I guess you know what I'm going to say."

Suddenly, to her horror, Leah *did* know what he was going to say! She wanted to cut him off, but he spoke before she could think of a way to do that.

"What I'm trying to say is that I just found out that you and Jeff aren't serious. If I'd known that before, I would have spoken earlier. But these last two weeks have been the best of my life. I've always liked you, ever since you came to Richmond, Leah. You know that. But I thought you and Jeff were . . . well . . . I thought you were in love. But now Jeff says you're not."

Leah gasped. "Cecil," she began, "I don't think—"

"I guess I want to say that I love you, Leah, and I'd like to be engaged to you."

Never had Leah Carter been so flabbergasted in her entire life! She sat with her hand held tightly in Cecil's hand, looking into his earnest eyes, and knowing that she had made a terrible mistake. Desperately she tried to think of some way to tell him.

He said, "This may come as a surprise to you, Leah, but I don't think so. I mean, after all, you've asked me over every day practically, and you wouldn't do that to a fellow unless you were serious, would you?"

Leah found herself nodding her head but all the time thinking, *No, no, it's all wrong!*

Cecil leaned forward suddenly and kissed her. "As soon as Jeff told me that there was nothing between you two, I knew what I had to do. You think about what I said, Leah, and I'll come back later."

Leah nodded, her throat so full she couldn't speak. She stood watching from the brook as Cecil mounted his horse, took off his hat and waved it at her, then rode off at a gallop.

Slowly she walked back to the house. Eileen spoke to her, but she did not answer. Instead she went straight to her room and sat down on her bed. And then she reviewed the history of what had happened between her and Cecil. The longer she sat there, the worse she felt.

At last she got up and sat at her desk. Taking out her journal, she dipped the turkey quill in ink and began to write:

I have made the most awful mistake of my life. I have made Cecil think I care for him—and I do, but not as he expects. He's just come to tell me he loves me and that he wants to marry me someday. Oh, what a fool I've been! What an utter, absolute fool. Jeff tried to tell me. Eileen tried to tell me. But I wouldn't listen!

Leah put the pen down and fell across the bed. Sobs racked her body. She was a sensitive, kind girl, but now she had hurt one of the dearest, most gentle young men that she had ever met. Guilt washed over her, and she could see no way out of the situation that she herself had created.

13
"With This Ring . . ."

The marriage of Col. Nelson Majors and Eileen Fremont took place in a small Methodist chapel. The building was filled, mostly with officers and men of the colonel's regiment.

"It sure looks odd," Jeff murmured, standing next to Tom at the front of the church. "Almost nobody here but men. Never saw a wedding like this."

"I guess that's the way it is in war time. There comes Leah."

Jeff looked back to see Leah, wearing a blue silk dress with a bow at her waist and a white hat tied beneath her chin. She held a bouquet and marched up the aisle steadily, then turned to stand beside him.

He nudged her and whispered, "You look great, Leah." He was surprised when her lips drew into a frown. *I wonder what's the matter with her,* he thought.

Across from Jeff and Tom stood their father. His ash-gray uniform was immaculate. Its brass buttons caught the glint of the lanterns burning on each side of the church and hanging from the chandeliers. He wore a scarlet sash around his waist, and he looked tall and straight and handsome. His eyes were fixed on the back of the church.

Suddenly Jeff saw him smile. The organ began to play "Here Comes the Bride," and all the officers and men turned to watch Eileen come down the aisle on the arm of the colonel's commanding officer. He had been delighted to give the bride away, although he was no relative.

Eileen was wearing a white dress—borrowed, Jeff knew. A long bridal veil fell down her back, and a sheer veil covered her face. She kept her eyes fixed on the groom. The lights were soft and the church quiet except for the sound of the organ.

The preacher asked, "Who gives this woman . . ." The general said, "I do," and there was the colonel standing across from her.

Jeff was fascinated as he watched. The two of them looked very handsome. He remembered with some shame how he had opposed the marriage. *She'll be a good wife to Pa,* he thought as the words of the wedding ceremony were spoken by the minister. *He needs someone. I know he's been lonesome, and she's already been a mother to Esther—and to me too.*

Finally the minister intoned, "By the authority vested in me, I pronounce you husband and wife." Then he smiled and said, "You may kiss your bride, colonel."

Nelson carefully lifted the veil from Eileen's face, bent over, and kissed her briefly. A cheer went up from his men, and the organ struck up the recessional.

Outside, officers quickly gathered to form a canopy of swords. The colonel and his bride passed underneath to where a carriage waited. He helped Eileen in, got in beside her, and then they waved at the cheering crowd.

"Let's get out of here, driver!" he said. "Before some of those fellows think up some tricks to play."

"Yes, suh."

The horses took off at a dead run.

Jeff laughed to see the carriage careening down the street.

"I reckon Pa was wise to get away," Tom said.

"He was, and they haven't told anybody where they're going for their honeymoon either. Pa said he was afraid somebody would think up a shivaree."

Then Jeff said, "And I guess we don't have to worry about Esther anymore."

"No." The look of relief on Tom's face and the sound of his voice showed how glad he felt. "She's a wonderful woman, Eileen is. Esther will have a great mother."

The two soldiers, looking strikingly similar, walked back into the church, where they were congratulated as though it were their own wedding.

"Look," Jeff said, "there goes Leah. She'll need some help taking care of Esther till Pa and Eileen get back. But we both have got to get back to Petersburg . . ."

Jeff hurried and caught up with her. "That was a good wedding, wasn't it?"

"Yes, it was."

Jeff looked at her questioningly. Leah was usually outgoing and bubbly, especially at a wedding. But then, he thought, she had been withdrawn and silent all day. "What's the matter with you, Leah?" he said. "Are you sick?"

"No, I'm all right. I just don't . . . feel much like talking."

He tried to get her to say more, but she said, "I've got to go home, Jeff. A neighbor is taking care of Esther, and I promised I'd come home early."

And off she went.

Leah ran upstairs to check on Esther and found her asleep. Then she went back downstairs and said, "Thank you so much for keeping Esther, Mrs. Dayton. I can take her now."

"Was it a nice wedding?" Mrs. Dayton asked. She was a woman in her late fifties with two boys in the Confederate army.

"Oh, yes, it was very nice. Colonel Majors looked very handsome and, of course, his bride was lovely."

"Such a romantic thing. They'll be so good for each other."

"Yes, they will," Leah said absently.

When the woman left, promising to return, Leah made herself a cup of tea. Then she sat at the kitchen table and drank it slowly. From time to time she heard people go by on the road. Sometimes a horse would pass at a gallop. At other times the groaning of wagon wheels came to her. She thought of Jeff and how she had cut him off almost without a word.

"It seems I can't do anything right," she said aloud and started at the sound of her own voice. *Here I am, starting to talk to myself!*

She got to her feet and did housework for a time. But her mind kept going back to Cecil. He had returned later on the day of his proposal. She had not felt able to talk with him, and he had left somewhat deflated. She knew that sooner or later he would be back.

She wandered into the backyard and leaned against the trunk of the apple tree and thought of how she had made such a terrible mess of things. She could only ask God to forgive her.

If only I'd never had that crazy idea of making Jeff jealous, she thought. *It seemed so harmless at the time,*

128

but now—how in the world am I ever going to tell Cecil the truth?

All afternoon she tossed the problem back and forth, trying to find some way out. She went upstairs and began a letter to Cecil. But though she started three of them, whatever she said sounded silly, or trite, or cruel. She threw down the quill and for the rest of the day took care of the little girl.

Leah slept fitfully that night and arose feeling drugged and miserable. After breakfast she spent part of the morning playing with Esther. She was fascinated by the golden-haired child and her patter and for a time was almost able to forget her problems.

At eleven o'clock, however, she heard a horse pull up outside. She went to a window, and her heart sank. "It's Cecil."

When Cecil entered, she knew that there could be no more putting off what she had to do.

"Hello, Leah," he said, smiling and removing his hat. "I'm sorry I haven't been able to come by, but they've kept me pretty busy at headquarters."

"That's all right."

"I think we can go out for a walk tonight. I believe I can get off. Maybe we can go get some more ice cream."

"Cecil . . . I've got something to tell you, and it's not going to be very easy."

He probably saw the trouble in her eyes. "What is it? Not bad news from home?"

"No, nothing like that . . . I . . . I got a letter from my brother, Royal. He's engaged to a girl in Atlanta. They're going back to Pineville after the war and get married there."

"Why, that's fine. Say, maybe you and I could go there too, and it could be a double wedding."

Leah saw the happiness in the lieutenant's thin face, and she swallowed hard. But she knew what had to be said.

"Cecil," she began slowly and with great difficulty, "I've always been fond of you. Ever since I came to Richmond. Even when I didn't behave very well, you were always kind to me. And I *didn't* always behave well."

"I don't know as I've noticed you misbehaving, Leah."

She shook her head impatiently. "Well, I have, and if you stop and think about it, you could remember a few times when I needed to be spanked. But now I've done something that I'm really ashamed of, and I've got to tell you about it."

Cecil looked bewildered. "What is it, Leah? You can tell me anything."

Leah forced herself to meet his eyes. "Cecil, I'm so honored that you've asked me to be engaged to you. It's the highest honor a man can pay to a girl— and I'll never forget what you've done." Taking a deep breath, she said stiffly, "But we can never be married, Cecil."

All the happiness went out of his face. He stared at her in disbelief. "But—but, Leah, I thought that you cared for me."

"I do like you—very much. We've been such good friends, but . . ."

His face seemed to collapse. "But, Leah," he said, "you've been so anxious to be with me the past few weeks. I thought that meant you cared."

She shook her head. "I do care. Very much, indeed. But in the first place, Cecil, with this war on, who knows how it will end, or where it will end? It's no time to be even *thinking* about marriage."

"The colonel did . . . and now you say your brother's going to get married . . ."

Trapped, Leah said, "I know, but they're older. I'm only seventeen. I know some girls get married at that age, but . . . well . . . I'm just not ready for that kind of commitment yet. And I don't think you are either, Cecil. I know you like me, and I like you. But it's just not time for things like that."

He stared at her, disappointment written all over him. "You're not telling me the whole truth, Leah. I can tell. There's something wrong with the way you look."

Then Leah knew that she had to tell him everything. She had confessed her wrong to God, but now she had to confess to this boy she had hurt so deeply. She hesitated only briefly. "I told you I don't always behave as I should, and I've done a terrible thing to you, Cecil. I made up to you to make Jeff jealous."

Cecil's thin face turned pale. For a moment he seemed to freeze.

"Oh, Cecil, I'm so sorry!"

"So you were just playing with me?"

"Don't put it like that!"

His lip quivered. He bit it then and straightened up. His voice was thin and filled with disappointment and hurt as he said, "I didn't think you would do that to me, Leah. I thought you were a different kind of person."

"Cecil—"

But the lieutenant wheeled and stalked off. The door slammed.

She ran after him. As she came out onto the porch, he was mounting, and she called his name. "Cecil, please don't go. Let me tell you—"

But Cecil was gone. He slashed his horse with the reins, and the animal reared, then shot forward in a wild burst of speed.

Leah watched as he disappeared, and her knees felt weak. She had never felt so miserable in all her life.

Lucy knew at once that something was wrong. She had gone to the Taylor house, as she often did, on a visit with her mother. She had been disappointed not to find Cecil there, but later that afternoon she saw him riding in and went out to meet him.

The lieutenant dismounted, handed the reins to a slave, and turned toward Lucy when she greeted him.

"Why, Cecil, what's the matter?"

"Nothing."

"There is too. You look awful!" She put a hand on his arm. "Come over here and sit down." She urged him into a secluded section of the yard formed by tall rose hedges. Then she sat down beside him. "What in the world is wrong with you? Your hands are trembling."

"I can't tell you."

Lucy was baffled. She tried to think of some awful thing that Cecil might have done that had so shaken him. She took his hand and held it in hers and said, "I don't care what you've done, Cecil. You can tell me. It won't go any farther. Maybe I can help."

"Nobody can help."

Perhaps it was the sympathy in Lucy's eyes and the touch of her hand on his that brought Cecil's defenses down. At any rate, he finally poured out the whole story, ending by saying, "She told me she was just seeing me to make Jeff jealous."

Lucy was shocked at the bitterness in his voice. She suddenly realized that Cecil Taylor was the kindest boy she had ever known. He had never hurt anybody in his entire life. Anger shot through her as she realized what Leah Carter had done. Hot words leaped to her lips—but she knew that was not what Cecil needed to hear.

"I'm sorry you had to go through this, Cecil," she said softly. She stroked his hand, thinking of the times he had comforted her when she had been foolish—which had been rather often. "I remember the time that I made such a pest of myself when I had that crush on David Jamison. It was you who came and helped me to see how silly I was being. How old was I—fourteen? And he was almost twenty?"

"I remember," he said.

"There were other times too. You've always been there when I needed you, and I wish now you'd let me be a friend to you."

Cecil looked down. "I even talked to Jeff. I asked him if he cared for her."

"What did he say?"

"He said that they'd been friends all their lives, but if I wanted to go calling on her that it was all right with him."

"He *had* to say that, don't you see? I think Jeff truly cares for her, and Leah does care for him. She's been a foolish girl, but then so have I been—many times."

Lucy talked gently for a long while, and slowly he seemed to relax. "I'd hate to see you become bitter over this, Cecil. Leah isn't a bad girl. She's just been foolish."

He slowly nodded. "I guess you're right." He forced a grin and said, "I'm glad you were here to pick up the pieces. I don't guess I would have shot myself or anything, but I was feeling pretty low."

Lucy leaned over and kissed him on the cheek. "Come on, let's go into the kitchen. Suzy made some chocolate cookies. You always liked chocolate cookies better than anything."

"All right."

Lucy led him away, thinking, *What a stupid girl Leah Carter is. I'd thought better of her.* Then she again remembered some of her own escapades and quickly added, *But I guess all of us make foolish mistakes. We just have to learn to deal with them.*

14

A Dress for Charlie

Rosie wandered along the streets of Atlanta, rather depressed by the sight. Most of the businesses were boarded up. Many had been destroyed by the shelling of Federal cannon. The citizens who passed him were poorly dressed and had a look of defeat written on their features. Many of them looked angrily at his blue Union uniform, and Rosie muttered, "I can't say I blame them much. If the Rebels had bombed out Pineville like we done with this place, I guess I'd be pretty mad myself."

For a time he roamed aimlessly along side streets, and then he came to a plate glass window that had miraculously remained intact. It was a dressmaker's shop, and the dress in the window caught his eye. It was a shade of peach, almost pink but not quite, and it made a vivid flash of color against the drabness of the grim buildings.

As Rosie looked at the dress, an idea began to form in his mind. He was not an impulsive young man, so he stood there until the whole thing was as clear as if he were seeing it in a photograph.

"By george, I'll do it!" he spoke aloud.

An old man hobbling along with a sack over his shoulder turned to give him a startled look.

Smiling, Rosie entered the shop. The showroom was no more than ten feet square. Two more dressmaking dummies stood inside, both adorned with rather plain dresses.

Across the door at the back of the shop hung a pair of dark green curtains. These parted, and a tall, gray-haired woman stepped into the main room. She looked at Rosie curiously, then said, "Yes, sir. May I help you?"

"Well, I'm interested in that dress in the window."

"Oh, yes. It's very pretty, isn't it?" The woman went to the window and lifted out the model. Setting it down, she said, "It's pure silk. The last bolt that got here before the siege. I had just enough to make this one dress."

"Sure is pretty. Kind of a peach color."

"You have someone you're thinking of buying it for?"

"Uh, yes, ma'am. I reckon I do. The trouble is, I don't know much about sizes."

"How large is the young woman?"

"Well . . . I guess about this tall."

"Is she thin?"

"No, ma'am. Not a bit of it!" Rosie protested.

"Well, without being offensive, is she . . . shall we say, heavy?"

Rosie shook his head. "Why, no, ma'am, she's just a good size."

The woman looked somewhat frustrated. "How old is she?"

"About eighteen years old."

"Sir, if you could get one of her other dresses, I might see if this dress would do for her."

Rosie grinned ruefully. "I don't reckon I could do that, ma'am. She's only got one dress. Don't think I could manage to get that one away from her."

"I should suppose not." She turned to the model. "This dress was made for a rather tall girl. She

136

ordered it, and then her family left Atlanta. If you'd bring the young lady in, I'd be glad to fit it for her."

"Would you now? That'd be right kind of you, ma'am, but I'm not sure I can get her to come in. She don't take much to dresses."

The dressmaker stared at him. "Doesn't take to dresses?"

"No, ma'am. She wears mostly overalls."

"Overalls. I see."

Rosie felt the situation was getting out of hand. He said, "Uh . . . how much do you want for the dress, ma'am?"

"Confederate money or Federal money?"

Rosie had just been paid two days earlier and had several months' pay in his pocket. "U.S. notes, ma'am."

Relief came to the woman's eyes. She named a price.

Rosie said, "That sounds fair enough. I'll tell you what. Why don't you let me take it with me, and then, if it don't fit, maybe you'd let her bring it back and you could take it in or let it out? Whatever it might need."

"I'll be happy to do that. Here, let me wrap it up for you."

Ten minutes later, Rosie was on the street, walking along with a brown package under his arm. His lips were moving as he spoke to himself. "I don't rightly see how I can handle this all by myself. I guess I better go get Miss Lori to help me with it."

"It's a beautiful dress, Rosie," Lori said. She held it up against herself and looked down. "I don't know as I ever saw a prettier one."

"Do you think she'll like it?" Rosie shifted from one

foot to another. His idea had seemed sound enough before he bought the dress, but now it seemed rather foolish.

"If she doesn't, she'd be an unusual girl."

"Charlie *is* unusual, as you know, Miss Lori. She don't go in for fine dresses and things like that."

"No, she doesn't. What made you think of buying her a dress?"

"Well, this is the first of October. Next Friday there's going to be a ball. The officers got it up for the enlisted men. So I thought that maybe if Charlie would put this dress on and kind of pretty herself up, why, she might catch Drake's attention."

Lori suddenly lowered the dress. Concern came into her eyes. "I heard about the fight you had with Drake."

"Yes, ma'am, I did. But you know Drake's done hit the glory trail."

Lori's lips turned up into a smile. "Yes, I've heard that too. Royal told me he's had a real change of heart."

"He sure has, ma'am. I've known Drake since he was just a shaver, and—I hate to say it—but he was pretty much of a buster. Always lookin' out for himself. When he told me he had gotten himself converted, I almost couldn't believe it. But he's been real different. He told me he's apologized to Charlie."

"Yes, he did. She told me about it. It helped her feelings a lot."

"But she ain't never going to catch him if she doesn't get out of them overalls and put on something pretty and frilly and . . . well, like this. So I thought if she'd put it on, and you'd help her a little bit, and she went to that ball, and Drake saw her . . . don't you think that'd help her get him?"

138

Lori said suddenly, "Don't you ever think of yourself, Rosie?"

He stared at her with astonishment. "Why would I want to be thinkin' about myself?"

"I mean, you're very fond of Charlie yourself."

Rosie felt himself blush. "I've always thought Charlie was a fine young lady."

"Have you told her so?"

"Uh . . . yes!"

"Have you really?" Lori persisted. "I mean, have you ever *really* told her that you admire her—and think that she's a fine young lady?"

"Well, I told her I liked the way she hunted possums."

"Rosie, how impossible you are!"

"Anyway, she's got her head and her heart set on Drake."

"I'd not be too sure about that."

"I know her, and I've talked to her a lot. Anyway, will you help her get ready for the ball?"

"Of course I will, but you and I will do it together. I want her to know what you're doing for her."

"I guess that'll be all right. Don't see no harm in it."

"Let me go get her. She's out back."

Rosie stood nervously in the sitting room and once almost turned and fled. "She doesn't need me to help with this, Miss Lori don't," he muttered. And then he wheeled about and faced the two women as they entered the room.

"Now," Lori said, "tell Charlie what you've come up with."

"It's not much," Rosie said. "But . . . uh . . . I saw this dress in the window, and I thought since there's a party comin' up—a sort of ball—that you might

139

put it on and go. And I come to get Miss Lori to help you pretty up and fix your hair and things."

Charlie stared at Rosie in astonishment. When he finished his stumbling explanation, she asked quietly, "Why did you do this, Rosie?"

"I . . . well, I know how set you are on catchin' Drake, and I bet you if he sees you in this pretty dress, he'll just plain come over to your way of thinkin'."

Charlie looked over at Lori, who was smiling at her, and her own lips began turning up at the corners. She said, "You're a sweet boy, Rosie." She pulled his head down and gave him a resounding kiss. "It's about the nicest thing anybody ever done for me in my whole life!"

Rosie whirled toward the door. "Shoot, it wasn't all that much." He looked back, saying, "I'll be sure Drake's at that ball. You get that dress on now and make sure it fits." And then he was gone.

Lori watched Charlie pick up the dress, feel its silky texture, and hold it against her cheek.

"I can't do it, Lori," she said.

"Why not?"

"It's just not right. I see that now. I been wrong the way I been going after Drake."

Lori said at once. "Yes, you have been. But you're going to that ball, and you're going to let Drake see what he's been missing. And every other young man at that party will see a beautiful young lady."

Rosie said nothing to Drake until the night before the ball. They were sitting in front of their tent

140

watching the stars spangle the sky like bright pin-points of light against a velvety black cloth.

"Them stars sure is pretty," Rosie said. "It seems to settle my stomach down just to look at 'em. Better than Dr. Smith's Antiseptic for Heartburn."

Drake grinned at his friend. "Yes, it's nice out here."

And then Rosie said, "Do me a favor, Drake."

"Anything you ask, Rosie."

"You know that ball the regiment's havin'?"

"Sure, it's tomorrow night."

"Well, I want you to go along with me. There's a little gal I got my eye on, and I want you to kind of help me. You can go over and meet her, and then you can introduce me and then sort of fade out."

Drake laughed. "Why don't you do it yourself?"

"Oh, I'm not good at things like that. But it'll be easy for you." Rosie felt somewhat deceitful about tricking Drake. "Will you do it, partner?"

"I'll be glad to. We'll have to dress up. Put on our finest duds. I'd like to see this girl you're so inter-ested in. Never knew you to take out after girls much."

"This one's kind of special. I'll bet you'll have a good time too. Bring your fiddle along, and you can join the other musicians."

Drake said, "Might could."

Rosie studied Drake's face secretly and then said, "You sure are different. I never saw a man make such a turnaround."

"I guess I needed a turnaround more than most," Drake remarked quietly. "I been a pretty sorry ex-cuse for a man."

"I was real proud to see you get baptized. I think every man in the regiment was there."

Drake laughed. "I guess they were. They couldn't believe that Drake Bedford was interested in God. I feel good about it, Rosie. First time in my life I feel all right. I made a lot of mistakes along the way, but I'm trustin' Him now. Ever since I called on the Lord Jesus out there in those woods, I've had peace inside."

At bedtime, Rosie said, "All right, don't forget. You got to go to that girl and introduce me to her."

"Sure. And we'll fix you up till you look like a major general. We'll get some French perfume and put on you so she can't resist you."

"That's the ticket." Rosie grinned.

Rosie lay in the darkness thinking, *Hate to set old Drake up like this*. He thought of Charlie then. But the thoughts he framed he would not speak aloud.

15
The Prettiest Girl
at the Ball

The last rays of the afternoon sun pierced the windows of the Holcomb house, illuminating the dress of the girl standing in the middle of the room. The dress was a light peach color, almost pink, and made of the finest silk. The neckline was low, round, and off the shoulder, edged with delicate white lace. The tight-fitting bodice had a series of white silk ribbon bows, decreasing in size down to the waist. The oval-shaped skirt was full and plain, except at the bottom, where two rows of the same soft white lace encircled the base of the dress.

"Oh, Lori, I've never seen anything like it!"

Lori, kneeling, took a final stitch in the hem. Then she stood and stepped back to admire her handiwork. The dress had fit almost perfectly, but she had made some slight improvements. This afternoon she had styled Charlie's hair so that the girl looked completely different. Instead of falling in wild curls, now it was piled high on her head into a large chignon, loosely braided and held in place by a pair of ivory combs. A few brown curls had escaped the combs and formed a soft frame around her face.

"You look absolutely ravishing!"

Charlie stirred uneasily. "I feel foolish!" she blurted out. She turned to look at herself in the mirror and stopped dead still. "I do look different," she muttered.

"You surely do. You look like a young lady going to a ball."

"I don't want to go to that old party," Charlie said abruptly. "I don't know how to act."

"You don't have to 'act' as good as you look. Just stand there in the ballroom and smile. All those young fellows will fall over themselves to come to you."

"But they'll want me to dance, and I don't know how!" Charlie wailed.

"Just tell them that you don't feel like dancing but you'll sit with them or walk around the ballroom with them. They'll be happy, believe me, for any attention you give them."

At that moment a knock sounded on the door.

"There. That'll be Royal coming for us. He's going to see that you get there and that you get home safely."

Lori ran to the door, opened it, and Royal grinned at her. "Is Cinderella ready?"

"I think she is. Come and look at her."

Royal put his arms around Lori and gave her a resounding kiss. "You'll be the prettiest girl at the ball," he whispered.

"No, I won't either. Look at Charlie."

She hauled Royal into the sitting room, and when he saw Charlie in her beautiful dress, his eyes flew open. "Well, I wish to my never," he said. "Miss Charlene, you are a dream."

"Oh, you hush, Royal! You're just makin' fun of me!"

"I am not. Indeed, I am not! I've got the two most beautiful young ladies at the ball right in my

144

keeping. We'll show them how to have a ball in this town."

"And Drake will see something he's never seen before," Lori whispered.

"Where is this girl you're so anxious for me to introduce you to?"

"I . . . uh . . . I don't see her right now," Rosie said nervously.

He and Drake stood at the entrance of the large, open building that had been turned into a ballroom. Decorations hung from the ceiling, and a military band was playing. Couples were already sweeping around the floor, and the dresses of the women made brilliant splashes of color. Rosie searched the room, then said, "She'll be here pretty soon."

The two soldiers joined others standing along the wall, watching.

"I'm surprised there's so many local girls here," Drake said. "But a party brings the ladies out, doesn't it?"

"Yeah, I guess it does." Rosie started to say something else, but at that moment he saw Charlie come through the door. "There she is. Right there!"

Drake's eyes opened wide. "She *is* a pretty thing. What's her name?"

"Uh . . . Suzie. Yes, Suzie."

"Suzie what?"

"Uh . . . just Suzie. Go on, Drake. Look—fellas are already gettin' ready to ask her to dance, but you go first. You know how to handle it."

"All right. Here I go."

Rosie watched as Drake walked across the floor. He admired the way his friend deftly sidestepped some of the soldiers who were edging toward Charlie, and he thought, *Here's your chance, Charlie. Make the most of it.*

Charlie had seen Drake at once and stood stock-still. When he came closer, she saw with some surprise that he was smiling at her.

And then he said, "Miss Suzie, may I have the honor of this dance?"

"Suzie?" She stared at him. "Why are you calling me Suzie?"

Drake blinked. "Isn't your name . . ." And then recognition came. "It's not—you're not—" he shook his head "—no, it couldn't be."

"Why are you talkin' so funny, Drake?"

"Charlie, it's you!"

A young sergeant came up and said, "Drake, if you aren't going to dance with this young lady, I'll do it."

"Never mind, sergeant," Drake said. "You were just going to dance with me, weren't you, Miss Satterfield?"

Before she could answer, he took her by the arm and led her away.

"Drake," she whispered, "I can't dance!"

"Of course you can," he said with confidence. "I'll help you, and we'll just sort of walk around the room." He took her free hand, held it out, and said, "Like this." He moved to one side slowly, and Charlie moved in the same direction. "That's the way. Now, again. We just sort of walk around."

Charlie had seen dancing before and had a natural rhythm. She was a little awkward at first, but soon she found the way of it.

Drake grinned with delight. "You're going to be a great dancer, Charlie."

146

"I didn't know I could do this." She was half dizzy as they swung around the room, but she found she could keep pace with him. She had hated the idea of coming to the ball and hated even worse the idea of facing Drake. Now she looked up and studied his face.

When he saw her eyes on him, Drake flushed and said, "I didn't think I'd ever be dancing with you, Charlie."

"No, we never talked about things like that. All I ever talked about," she said, "was farms, and mules, and things."

"I've—I've already told you how sorry I am. For the way I treated you."

"You don't have to say that every time we meet, Drake."

"I know, and I won't say it again. God's forgiven me, and I've asked you to, and I reckon you will."

Charlie nodded and murmured, "I sure do."

The music ended, and at once half a dozen young men came to claim Charlie. She clung to Drake's arm, however, and looked up at him with alarm, whispering, "Don't let them have me, Drake."

"Of course not. I'm sorry, gentlemen," he said louder, "but I have engaged Miss Satterfield for the next five dances."

There was a protest, but Drake said, "Come on, Charlie. Let's go get some refreshments."

He led her across the room, where they drank punch and ate small tea cakes.

Drake said, "You look beautiful. I really didn't know you when I first saw you tonight. I wish you'd throw those overalls away. A beautiful young woman like you should never wear anything but pretty dresses."

"It would be hard to plow with a dress like this."

"You won't be plowing, will you?"

"I hope so."

Drake looked at her quickly. "You still mean that about a farm, don't you?"

"I sure do."

"Well, I'm not a farmer. I already told you that." He smiled kindly. "But I feel real honored that you wanted me to marry you, Charlie, even though it never would have worked."

Charlie nodded slowly and put down her glass. "I know you're right, Drake. I see that now."

After two more dances with Drake, Charlie said suddenly, "Where's Rosie?"

Drake looked to the wall where he had left the tall soldier and laughed. "That son of a gun. I forgot him. He tricked me to get me to come to the ball." He told her how Rosie had schemed to throw the two of them together. "Rosie's a good friend—and he meant well—but he failed this time, didn't he?"

During the next two dances, Charlie thought hard about what Drake had said. She found that she was not enjoying dancing despite the attention of the young men. "I want to talk to Lori, Drake."

"All right. There she is—over there with Royal."

When they joined Lori and the sergeant, Drake said, "What do you think of our Charlie? Isn't she a beauty?"

"She sure is," Royal said. "One of the two prettiest girls at this ball."

"Lori, can I talk with you?"

"Of course, Charlie." Lori led her into a side room and said, "What's wrong?"

"I don't know. I just don't feel right."

"But Drake's dancing with you. He thinks you're beautiful."

"I know, but it's just not like I thought it would be." She wrung her hands and smoothed the front of the peach dress. "It's a beautiful dress, and I guess I'd like to wear dresses once in a while, but I made a mistake. I just don't belong with Drake, and I just don't feel good here at this ball. I want to go home."

"But you can't go home *now*, Charlie."

"I'll wait for you, but I don't want to dance anymore. I'll just wait here."

"You can't wait out here by yourself!"

"Yes, I can. You go on back and have a good time."

Lori drew Royal aside. "Charlie's very upset," she told him. "She wants to go home."

"What's wrong with her? She's got what she wanted."

"No, she hasn't. She sees now that Drake never was a good choice for her. Even though he's changed his ways, he's just not right for her. He's not what she needs."

"What *does* she need?"

"I think right now she needs Rosie. Have you seen him?"

"He was outside leaning against the building a few minutes ago."

"Go get him. Tell him to go to that room right over there. No, wait! Let me get Charlie."

Charlie was surprised to see Lori in the doorway and then to hear her say, "Come with me, Charlie."

"I don't want to dance."

"You're not going to dance. I found a better place for you to wait."

"Oh, that's good."

She followed Lori around the edge of the ball-room until they came to the outside door.

"You can wait out here—it's quiet and private."

"Well . . . all right . . . if that's what you want."

As soon as the door closed, Charlie saw the tall figure of a man lounging in the shadows. She stiffened and started to go back inside, but then a familiar voice said, "Why, Charlie, what are you doin' out here?"

"Rosie, is that you?"

"Sure is," he said and emerged from the darkness. "What's the matter? I saw you dancin' with Drake. He thinks you're pretty as a pair of red shoes with green strings. I can tell."

"I don't care. I don't like it in there, Rosie."

He appeared flabbergasted. "But it's what you wanted!"

"I don't know what I wanted, but I know one thing—I was wrong." A new assurance came over Charlie. She looked up at Rosie and said firmly, "Drake and I won't ever get hitched. He won't ever be a farmer. And I want my man to be a farmer."

"But . . . well . . . I don't know if I can do anything about *that*. A man's what he is."

"And a girl's what *she* is, and I'm just not the girl for him—and he's not the man for me."

Rosie stood motionless. "Are you sure about that, Charlie?"

"I sure am."

He took a deep breath. "Well, then I'll have to announce that I'm comin' courtin'."

Charlie smiled. "Are you really going to do that?"

"Sure am, now that I'm sure you don't want Drake."

"Do you like to farm, Rosie?"

"Nothin' better! Give me a pair of good mules and look out!"

"Me too!" She suddenly laughed. "Wouldn't it be funny if you and me got hitched some day, Rosie?"

"I reckon I'd laugh myself to death." He looked into her face for a moment. "You know what I promised my ma one time?"

"What did you promise her, Rosie?"

"I promised her I'd never kiss a girl the first time I was alone with her at a dance."

"Did you really?"

"Sure did." He hesitated, then said, "I reckon I'm gonna have to break my promise to Ma."

"Maybe it's not good to break a promise to your ma," she whispered.

"I'll explain it all to her sometime." He bent forward and kissed Charlie on the lips. "Now I'm an official suitor, I reckon. I think what I'll do is, I come courtin' for a while, and then I ask you to marry up with me, and then we wait a while, and then we get married."

"Is that the way it works?"

"It sure is. So right now we're in phase one. Come on inside. And any yahoo that tries to dance with you, I'll have to chastise him. Nobody's dancin' with my girl!"

"If you say so, Rosie."

"Look, Royal!" Lori said. "It's Rosie and Charlie. And look at her. She looks like she's just found a million dollars."

"I think she's found something better." Watching them, Royal said, "Wouldn't it be something if those two wound up getting married?"

151

"It *would* be something, and I wouldn't be a bit surprised!"

16

The End and
the Beginning

Mrs. Grace Holcomb died quietly in her sleep on October 12. At the funeral both Charlie and Lori wept. They had learned to love the old lady who had gone so quietly to meet her Savior.

"In a way," Lori said as they left the cemetery, "I think it's best."

"Why do you say that?" Charlie asked.

"Because things would never have been the same for her." As they walked slowly back toward the house, Lori explained. "You see, she grew up in Atlanta when it was a gracious city, prosperous and happy. She had her husband and her family, but all that's gone now."

"I reckon that's so," Charlie said. She was wearing a black dress that had belonged years ago to one of Miss Grace's daughters. Looking down at it, she thought hard. "And she was ready to go. She was in such bad pain sometimes, and now she's out of all that."

When they were back at the house, Charlie asked, "What'll you do now?"

"I expect I'll have to go back to Tennessee."

Charlie bit her lip. "I don't know what I'll do. I guess I'll just stay here."

But Royal and Rosie came bursting in late that afternoon.

"You've got to get out of Atlanta at once!" Royal said.

"What's wrong, Royal?" Lori cried.

"The order's been given to burn Atlanta to keep the Rebels from occupying it again. Things are going to be pretty bad. Let's go. Right now!"

"But I can't leave Charlie here!"

"You're going too, Charlie!" Rosie said.

"Going *where?*"

"It's all settled," Rosie said. "Both of you are going back to Pineville. You know—that's my hometown. Mine and Royal's and Drake's. And Lori's aunt and uncle live there. You're gonna wait there until the war's over."

"And that won't be very long," Royal said with some assurance. "You'll take care of her, won't you, Lori?"

"Of course, I will." Lori put an arm around the girl and said, "We'll wait for our men together, won't we, Charlie?"

Charlie looked up at Rosie. "Is that what you want, Rosie? You want me to wait for you?"

"Sure do. And while you're waitin'—" he grinned "—you can be lookin' around for some blue-nosed mules. When we get that farm started, we'll need at least six, I'd say. Two for me, and two for you, and two to spell the others."

The exodus of the two girls from Atlanta was hurried. The men put them on the last train to leave before the city was put to the torch. As the train pulled out, they were both hanging out the window waving good-bye.

"I'll be waitin' for ya," Charlie said. "I'll have the mules all picked out."

154

"And I'll be waiting for you, Royal. No mules, but I'll be there."

The two soldiers watched the train leave the station, and Royal said with some relief, "I'm glad they got out. Things won't be good here."

"How long do you think this war will last? I'm kinda anxious to meander back to Pineville now to start my courtin'."

"Petersburg can't hold out much longer. As soon as it falls, Richmond falls, and then the war's over."

On the walk back to camp, Rosie was quiet for a while, then he said, "Imagine. I get Charlie, and a farm, and six blue-nose mules. Ain't that somethin', Royal?"

Royal slapped his friend on the back. "That's something, all right. I wish we were going back to Pineville tonight—but first we've got to finish off the fighting."

17

Jeff Has a Visitor

The steel net that Gen. Ulysses S. Grant had thrown around Petersburg constantly closed tighter. The Union lines extended farther and farther, encircling the city. Continually supplied by reinforcements, the Northern lines were thick and armed with the latest weapons. The Confederates had no new weapons, and their thinning ranks meant that every man had to cover more territory. Inside Petersburg, things could not have been much worse. In that city —and in Richmond as well—food supplies were practically gone.

Leah, however, found herself feeling so guilty over what she had done to Cecil Taylor that she scarcely noticed the end was drawing near. She had not heard from Royal since the news came that he was engaged. Nor had she been able to get letters from home or send any out. She helped care for Esther and spent much time with Eileen. Since Eileen had come back from her four-day honeymoon, the two had become very close. But even now, nothing Eileen said could make her feel better.

Sitting at the desk in her room one afternoon, she listened to Esther's merry voice sound from downstairs. *At least we don't have to worry about Esther not having a mother anymore. She's got a fine one,* she thought.

She opened her journal. There was a somber look on her face as she read over entries going all the way back to the first time that she had said, "I'm going to use Cecil to make Jeff jealous." She continued to read, and her face flamed as she realized again how wrong she had been. At last she took up her pen and began to write a new entry:

October 30, 1864. The city is falling apart, and the Yankees will soon be here. But I can't even make myself care. I worry about Royal, and I worry about Jeff, and his father, and Tom. I just want this awful war to be over. I haven't seen Jeff since I talked to Cecil. I know Cecil hates me, and I don't blame him a bit. Now Jeff will hate me. If I could only do it all over again!

She put the quill down and closed the journal.

Downstairs, she sought out Eileen. "I've got to do something."

Startled, Eileen looked up. "What is it, Leah?"

"I've got to go find Jeff."

"He's at Petersburg! You can't go to Petersburg. It's too dangerous!"

"I've got to talk to him about things, Eileen."

Eileen took the girl in her arms.

"I've just got to do it! I have to!"

"If you feel that strongly about it," Eileen said quietly, "then I'll get you there. We'll go down and get a carriage from the quartermaster corps, and we'll have a driver take you. What's the use of being the wife of a colonel if we can't get a favor now and then?"

"Do you think you could do it, Eileen?"

"I don't see why not."

Jeff was dozing in the trench when he felt his

shoulder shaken. He woke up, startled. "What is it?" he cried and almost jumped up.

"Stay down, Jeff! You want to get your head shot off?"

"What is it?"

"You got a visitor," the soldier said. "Keep your head down and go back behind the lines."

"Who?"

"Don't know. Word just came from the lieutenant for you to get back there."

"Thanks, Syd."

Jeff crawled until he was away from the front line. Then he straightened up and made his way to regimental headquarters, where he saw his father standing with a woman. She was wearing a cloak, and at first he thought it was Eileen.

I wonder what she's doing here, he said to himself. But when he got closer and the woman turned, he stopped in surprise. "Why, Leah!"

"A visitor for you, Jeff," Colonel Majors said. "She came all the way through the lines. My wife commandeered a wagon, and used my name, and wrote a pass and signed it. What do you think of that?"

"I guess she must've had a pretty good reason, then."

"I just had to see you, Jeff," Leah said.

The colonel said, "You two go in the tent. It's a bit too public out here."

"Yes, sir."

He led Leah inside and closed the tent flap. He lit the lamp and only then turned to her. "What's the matter?"

"Jeff, I just had to come." Leah slipped out of her cloak and let it fall to the ground. "I can't sleep. I can't eat. Everything is all wrong!"

158

"What in the world is it?"

"It's—it's the way I treated Cecil."

Relief washed over Jeff. "I thought Esther was sick or somethin' terrible like that."

"It *is* terrible!" Leah insisted, and her eyes seemed enormous in the lamp light. "It's terrible for *me*, Jeff."

He stared down at her. "Here, sit down on the cot and tell me all about it."

And she did.

"So you see I've been awful, Jeff," Leah moaned. Clasping her hands together, she squeezed them until her knuckles turned white. "I wish I could die, and I don't know why I did it." Tears gathered in her eyes. Her voice quivered. Her lip trembled. "Jeff, I'm such an awful person. Can you forgive me?" Then the tears spilled over, and she sobbed.

Taken off guard, he put an arm around her and stroked her hair, murmuring he did not know what.

When the sobs began to lessen, she straightened up. "I—I don't even have a handkerchief."

"Take this one." He pulled a handkerchief from his pocket. "It's clean. You can keep it."

Leah wiped her tears away, then looked at him and asked timidly, "Do you hate me, Jeff?"

"Hate you? Of course, I don't hate you."

"But Cecil does."

"No, he doesn't. I talked to him just yesterday. He told me all about it."

"So you already knew. But he was so hurt, and I don't blame him!"

"Well, he got a pretty rough bump." Jeff suddenly smiled. "But I guess your fatal charms aren't as powerful as you think."

"Jeff, when I told him, he was so mad that I could see he hated me."

"He told me he did get pretty mad at first. But then he went and talked to Lucy."

"*Lucy?* He went and told *her* what I'd done?"

"I think she helped him a little bit. They've always been great friends, you know."

"I like *that!* Telling Lucy!"

"But you're telling *me* what you did!" Jeff protested. "What's the difference?"

"If you don't see the difference, I can't explain it to you!"

"Look, you wanted Cecil to feel better—well, he feels better. He likes Lucy. He always has. She's always liked him. I wouldn't be surprised but what they start seeing each other. What do you care? You didn't want him. You just wanted to make me jealous!"

Leah's face flushed, but she nodded. "That's right. See how awful I am?"

Jeff took the handkerchief from her hand and wiped the remaining tears from her face. "I don't think you're awful."

Leah looked up. "You don't?"

"No, I don't. I think you're pretty special."

"You don't really think that. Not after what I did."

"Aw, that can't be the worst thing you ever did, Leah," he teased.

"You can make light of it, but I'll never forget it, and I'll never do anything like that again!"

As they sat talking, Leah calmed down. Then she stood and said, "I've got to go back. But I feel much better."

"I wish I could go with you." He got up too, looking around as if he could see through the sides of the tent. "Lines are going to cave in any day."

"What will happen then?"

"I don't know. But it'll all be over, I think. There's nothing between here and Richmond to stop Grant. And when Richmond falls—and the Army of Northern Virginia—the war's over."

"I wish it were over right now."

"So do I, but I'll have to stay in uniform until it is."

Shyly Leah put her hand on his chest. "Jeff, I'm really sorry about what I did. But I did it because . . . well . . . I didn't like the way you were paying attention to Lucy. But if you want to pay attention to her, that's all right."

"I got no intention of paying attention to Lucy." He put a hand over hers. "You know what?"

"What, Jeff?"

"You're not a little girl anymore. You're a young lady."

"Do you really think so?"

"Sure do. Now listen—if the army has to run away from the Yankees, I'll have to leave you in Richmond. Pa will have to leave Eileen there too. I may not see you again for a while."

Leah said, "I wish it wasn't that way." Suddenly she pulled his head down and firmly kissed his cheek. "There," she said.

She turned to leave, but he caught her hand. "That was a big girl kiss," he said. "A young lady type kiss. How old are you again?"

"You know how old I am! I'm seventeen, and you're eighteen."

"My, we're gettin' kind of old, aren't we? The first thing you know, I'll have a long white beard and you'll have a cane to walk with and an ear trumpet. Won't that be somethin'?"

161

Leah began to laugh. Jeff could always make her laugh. She reached up and touched his cheek. "Good-bye, Jeff. I'll be praying that God will keep you safe."

"Good-bye, Leah. God is going to take care of us."

He followed her out of the tent and watched as she got into the carriage. She waved, and the carriage rolled away.

"You and Leah get something settled, son?"

Jeff turned around to see his father and Tom. "I guess we did, Pa. We settled our differences. We're both growin' up."

Colonel Majors put a hand on his son's shoulder. "You're growing taller, Jeff, but you're growing inside too. And that Leah, she's going to be a fine one. Already is, as a matter of fact."

The Majors men watched the carriage disappear into the distance, and then the colonel said, "Well, back to the lines. We've got to hold as long as we can."

"We'll do that, colonel," Tom said. "Come on, Jeff. I'll walk back with you."

Colonel Majors watched his two sons walk away, and he breathed a silent prayer: *God, let it be over soon!*

The Bonnets and Bugles Series includes: